STRANGER
on
STRANGER

G.B. Hope

Stranger on Stranger

a work of fiction by GB Hope ©

Published by Bronwyn Editions in UK 2012

www.bronwyneditions.co.uk

ISBN: 978-0-9570745-0-7

Cover design by Jon Parris

Printed by Lightning Source UK 2012

A copy of this book has been sent to the British Library for legal deposit

To Caroline

Never mind, I'll find someone like you

PROLOGUE

That manic woman, who always walked fairly briskly while pushing an imaginary wheelbarrow, hustled by on the part of the High street visible to me from my position in the bath tub. In a week of total madness, I found the sight of her strangely comforting.

The warm bathwater complemented wonderfully the cool breeze coming through the open window. I doused my still frazzled head from a sponge and took a moment to again wonder how the hell I had gotten myself into this situation. Then, blowing water from under my nose, I looked out again. Next along the street came the woman who ran the hairdressing salon, cycling on a rusty boneshaker, complete with wicker basket on the front and wearing just the worst kind of Betty Grable hairstyle. Then the other way went that ruddy-faced man in the fluorescent workman's top who always walked on the road and never the pavement. They're all out today, I thought.

I received Beth lying back into me, her long silken legs alternately lifted to examine her shaving efforts. My chin rested on her right shoulder, allowing an overview of her wet breasts, with her blonde hair unusually down and lank, her young face still puffy from crying. She placed my arms around her taut midriff, my loins barely contained against her lower back.

'Are you all right now?' I asked softly.
'Much better, thank you.'
'Good.'
She had been found sitting on the outside metal stairs to my flat after another one of my fruitless visits to Candlesby; another adrenalin-fuelled, disturbing bicycle trip to that small Surrey village, but this time returning to the sight of the perfectly formed Beth with her knees pulled up to her chin and a smile made wonderful by the black eyes and the famous dimples in the cheeks. She was wearing denim shorts and a white tee-shirt. I liked the way her small white Reeboks were turned in at the toes. I took a look at her rust-bucket Mini parked there as if it lowered the tone.
'Hi,' I said.
'Hi, Alex.'

The clean summer morning and beautiful countryside had not escaped my admiration as I cycled along, wearing recently bought baseball cap and green train spotter's cagoule, with rucksack over my shoulders. As I turned the gear, I made the decision that it was best to become imbecilic; to be a boy crossing the playground to punch a rival, to be a driver doing sixty past a line of parked cars. Imbeciles do not use up emotional energy and I would need all that strength on the journey back. Even so, I started to feel wired, sweating in spite of the slow revolutions of the pedals, almost glad when the rain started and hammered off the cagoule and soaked the hat to my head. I watched the persistent rain against the backdrop of green and black. Green and black. Rain was good, rain stopped people looking at people, kept dogs waiting to be walked; nothing happened in rain.

But the rain stopped when I arrived in Candlesby. There were two women talking outside the chemist shop and a mother and child skipped through the puddles towards the newsagents. Water ran in rivers either side of the disused Post Office. I went up the right fork, up The Mount, weaving between water-filled potholes, bringing the smog mask up from inside the cagoule to cover my face. It was there, blue Saab! Blue Saab! Then down the public footpath and round the back of the cane furniture factory. Even with the difficult to handle thin wheels of the racer I circled round quickly to the main street, returning up The Mount. This time I stopped adjacent to Mathers' residence, to *Squirrel's Chase* as the man liked to call it, seeing a drenched stationary horse, but no human activity anywhere.

Now the rain had stopped, the birds started up. I moved around the boundary of *Squirrel's Chase* to find what I was looking for: a blind spot of foliage to hide me from the four nearest houses but which left a view through to Mathers' garage. I swung around the rucksack, removed the handgun and let it sag heavily into the front pocket of the cagoule.

The brown horse slowly came over to see me. I rubbed its damp face, playing the part of resting cyclist. I got about forty minutes out of the horse, strangely upset for not thinking of bringing an apple or something. Gratefully the sun had appeared to remove some of the wetness from my legs. Despite having the best spot, I thought it necessary to do some laps of the factory, if not least to get my blood going again.

First time round; no change. Second time; no, still Mathers seemed in for the day. I started to feel pangs of isolation. Another half hour passed. Not wanting to outstay my welcome or push my luck, I decided to retreat.

I thought on the way home about pushing my luck. I was looking for outrageous fortune. Or was I? What were my alternatives? Press the buzzer, say "parcel for Mr Mathers" and pose into the security camera? Approach the man in obviously public areas? No, I would try again tomorrow. The handgun was back in the rucksack and I headed out of Candlesby.

Arriving back at the flat, it no longer came as a surprise that I had a visitor. Perhaps it was something I should bank on for my next trip to Candlesby. What I didn't expect was Beth. I noted for the first time that her hair was not in its customary ponytail and that she looked drained. After exchanging greetings, I asked the obvious question, 'Looking for Tim?'

'Yeah, has he been here?'

'Not that I know. I've been exercising for a few hours.'

'I've really done it this time, Alex. I accused him of going with someone else.'

I was thinking of what I needed: a shower, some food, a re-charge of the batteries. I had never seen Beth look so vulnerable. How could I flippantly advise her to find the boy and make up? 'Come in,' I said. 'We'll talk.'

I let her in and, like all modern girls, she needed no invitation to make herself at home. She grabbed a mini-can of coke from the fridge, the trainers came off and she flopped down onto the sofa. First thing first, the rucksack with the handgun went into a cupboard. Shower and food, I needed shower and food, but Beth sat clearly waiting for my consultation. I sat down facing her, more taken than usual with the symmetrical perfection of her face which was aided by gradually lengthening strands of blonde hair.

'I just sensed something,' she started, 'from him, and then he looked all guilty. I went off my head. You know what I'm like, well, of course you know what I'm like.'

'Have you got any proof, Beth? A long brunette hair in his bed? A mystery text on his phone?'

'No, no. He was just odd with me, you know.'

'You didn't hit him, did you?'

'No.'

She threw herself back on the sofa, scraping up her hair in frustration and then letting it go in disgust. Her eyes glassed over.

'I love him to death, Alex. Maybe he did get up to something, but it doesn't really matter. I just feel so bad freaking on him again. I promised to stop being mad, because he is lovely, isn't he? Oh, and I'm sorry for hitting you and all.'

A tear dropped onto one of her babyish cheeks, prompting me forward, intending to hold her, but thinking better of it, instead wiping the tear away. Still my hand finished in her blonde locks and her head needingly sank onto it. Then it was she who held onto me, like a soft girl for a change instead of strong-willed young woman. Minutes went by.

'Is that where you play ball?' she asked over my shoulder. 'Tim said you played ball in the house like a little boy.'

'That's good of him. It's very cathartic. When do you ever see me stressed?'

She sat up.

'Go and shower,' she told me. 'You smell of damp and sweat.'

I smiled and stood. I almost said "come in with me", paused, shocked at my own outrageous shittyness with my "sister-in-law". 'Chill,' I said instead, for the first time in my life.

Showered and refreshed, I jumped onto the sofa next to her with *Ice Station Zebra* playing on TCM. I neglected to ask why she was watching Ice Station Zebra on TCM.

'Am I disturbing anything?' she asked. I shook my head. 'Have you got anything for tea?'

'I'll sort something out.'

I waited for Patrick McGoohan's table banging scene before going for a glass of juice. She turned to watch me, nodding when I offered a glass.

'Shall I call Tim?' I asked.

'*Why*?'

'So I can feel important. I'll tell him you're at my place. That I'm dealing with it. I'm sorting you out.'

'Are you sorting me out?'

I smiled. 'Do I have to?' I returned to my seat. 'Listen,

you could just remember what happened between us when I first came down this neck of the woods. Then, Beth, sweetheart, whether or not a stoned Tim got friendly somewhere with some stoned girl or not, you can just get on with loving the loveable chap.'

She mimed a "wow, that gave it to me straight".

'There you are, done,' I said. 'What would you like for tea?'

Actually, I hadn't done much shopping recently. We continued to talk about everything and nothing, we shot some pool on the most important feature of the flat, then crashed out in the lounge area with pizza and wine. After the meal she changed position to be facing down to my up, going on with herself about Tim, constantly pushing her hair behind her ears. I contentedly lay there, with little Beth, adorable, this moody creature, the light seemingly allowing me into her black eyes.

She stopped talking. 'What are you thinking about?'

'Pleased you're here.'

Her jaw dropped. 'Yeah, like you're ever short of company. Where's the new love, then?'

'I told her never to disturb me when there's a knackered Mini outside.'

She sank down onto her hands, big fresh whiter than white globes staring at me. I couldn't resist scraping her hair back. 'My look,' she said.

'You know what, Beth. I wish I'd met you at school. I'd have battered... Kenny... Lewis to go out with you and we'd have been inseparable.'

'And we grow up together.'

'Yeah, you briefly leave me for an Australian bartender, but then we live happily ever after. I think that's been my problem. Chasing the love I should have had. And I've always been out of sync with the girls ever since. Wanting commitment when they wanted clubs. Looking for romance when they were looking for furniture.'

'Now you've got this Joely girl.'

'Yeah, she gives me that feeling inside. That indescribable feeling. I've had that once before.'

'What, when you first met me?'

'No, that'll be a different feeling.'

She smiled.

'God, I feel so grubby,' she said. 'Do I look a mess?'

I considered my answer, not wanting to suggest she could shower while she was there. 'You look... a little tired, that's all.'

'Oh, I look terrible, don't I?'

She sat up with a sigh, deciding what to do for the best.

'Alex, will you wash my hair?'

I gestured at being uncomfortable with that.

'Please, Alex. It's only washing my hair.' She played on my discomfort. 'I'll just bend over the bath.'

I happily despaired of her, grabbing her legs. 'Why are you here, Madam? Because you're upset about Tim. Now you want some other guy to wash your hair.'

'You're not some other guy, Alex. What's wrong? You've done it before, and as I remember it was lovely.'

I ran my fingers through my own hair before caressing hers, wanting to wash it for her, knowing that I would, despite immediately chastising myself.

'I'll go home to get cleaned up, then.'

I heaved her to her feet.

'Come on, I'll wash your hair. But that's all.'

Beth giggled and hugged me from behind, walking with me in that position to the bathroom.

I set the shower head running down into the side of the bath, remembering how I liked washing women's hair, or indeed just playing with women's hair. Beth removed her top, dropping it in my field of vision. Then she turned the handle to close the bathplug.

'What's this?' I asked.

'Can't we bathe while you wash my hair?'

'Beth, you're incorrigible.'

I watched the slow bend back down to open the taps, those black eyes naughtily daring me, lank blonde hair behind an ear, lacy pink bra above soft white torso.

'Alex, what?'

'I should throw you out.'

The water powered into the stained old bathtub, more cold than hot to allow for the warm day.

'I just need to be held, Alex.'

'Nothing more?'

'I swear. Let's set some ground rules, if you like.'

'Such as?'

'Well, we're just to enjoy the water, and the leisurely, very leisurely washing of my hair, and I might shave my legs...' I oohed at that. 'And you can't take me up...'

I stopped her with a fingertip to her lips.

'No messing about, Beth. Let's just be nice. If you want more than nice you can go now.'

'Nice will do.'

I took over the filling duties while she stripped in my peripheral vision. Then she settled down into the water with a few splashes around her chest. I lessened the power of the shower before quickly discarding my clothes to slide in behind her, immediately receiving her leaning back into me with a sigh.

We softly waffled on about nothing in particular while I played with her hair, then she asked for a razor. I reached up above my head to provide a bic for her to shave her legs.

'Shall I shave you?' she asked.

'My stubble's too thick for a razor.'

'Really?' She turned to have an unsuccessful scrape of my chin.

'Told you.'

While she was arched forward to do her shins I soaped her back with careful circles, savouring the closeness. I used the showerhead to rinse her off, then slipped my hands around to her tight tummy to lever her backwards. At first she resisted with her ablutions unfinished, leaving me to view the street below.

When she relaxed onto me I immediately vetoed any guilty debate between myself and my conscience and with soapy hands began to fondle her, Beth all relaxed and mildly delirious.

'Don't stop,' she said.

It was impossible for me not to become aroused against her lower back as I moved from excited breasts down to her tight bellybutton, around her smooth hips on

the waterline and back up to resume firm soaping.
'Such a babe,' I said to her right ear.
'I know.'

ONE

I was always under the impression there were many pleasant ways to be woken up in the morning: a favourite tune on the radio, the sound of birdsong, the aroma of bacon and eggs, a blonde woman blowing in your ear, or somewhere else for that matter.

Finally I stirred, suffering summer's glare through the flimsy curtains, terribly dehydrated with the window shut after a previous night's threesome with wasps from the nest in the roof. I was also aware of emerging from one of those physically draining dreams, although it had ceased too early to be brought clearly to mind. There was noise as well. The running water of my shower with some tuneless bitch singing under it was not too annoying, but she was in competition with *Eminem* emanating from the High street.

I propped myself up on my elbows to excavate my eyes. I think it was a Tuesday, early August, working late shift, a little unhappy at the thought of that, but as I was more or less my own boss there was no real cause for complaint. In fact, my life was as ordered and content as it had been in a long time. Two girlfriends had departed with the minimum of fuss: first the shoplifter from Watford and then the asylum seeker from Romania. Finally I was out of debt, had some good friends around me and liked this normally quiet part of the world. Who *was* that in the shower?

She came through in just a towel and informed me that I was awake, thank you very much. I liked the delicate toned shoulders and the bouncy walk to look out to see where the noise was coming from. She looked good for forty with a somewhat unusual boys' crew-cut that was already nearly dry. Her name was Nichola Duckinfield and this had been our first night together after her rather amateurish campaign to secure herself a toy boy, albeit a twenty-eight-year-old one who only had to be asked.

'There are illegal immigrants getting out of the back of a truck,' she reported.

'It's all right. I live above a Chinese Takeaway.'

She turned, nice teeth, the only hint of her age being around her eyes. The bed sheets had long since been kicked off and she seemed to be trying not to ogle my bare behind. I smiled to myself. She really was a lovely woman, despite being obscenely loaded. I was quite happy to let her look at me, knowing my backside to be white with the rest of me being golden brown and impressively toned. Breaking the pose and dragging myself to my feet had her a little flustered with her eyes guiltily focussing, before she turned back to the window.

I moved in behind her, wrapping my arms around her slender body, squashing her breasts upwards. She sighed back into me.

'Do you get any free food?' she asked.

'I do, but I don't really like Chinese. I should have taken the flat above the Italian down the road. Are you aware that you're digging your nails into my arse?'

'Sorry.'

We both laughed and then I padded off to the bathroom, calling, 'Give me a minute and I'll sort out some breakfast.'

She was dressed and with her belongings gathered when she came to lean on the bathroom door. As the previous tenant had seen fit to take the shower curtain she was now watching me shower.

'I can't stay,' she said. 'My husband, Neil, and my son fly into Heathrow within the hour.'

I played it quietly cool, not wanting to say "Okay, 'bye, then". So I let the lukewarm jet hit my face until she had to say it.

'Okay, 'bye, then.'

'Yeah, 'bye, Nichola.'

'Will I see you again?'

I said, 'Of course,' trying to sound sincere.

She smiled her nice smile and went to collect her family.

I dressed in shorts and tee-shirt, stepped into my Fila mules and clanked down the metal stairs into the morning heat. My Landlord and new friend, Mike Yu, was there with three of his sons and a tonne of deliveries. A happy fifty-year-old Chinese man, he was smiling as always as he came to speak to me.

'Hey, Alex, I liked that one. She's always welcome.'

We paused while a train sped through on the track behind the shops.

'You liked that one, did, you?'

'Oh, yeah. And her car, a brand new convertible Merc.

Very nice.'

On that topic I had a good look at my black Audi A3. It was third-hand but was still the best car I had ever owned. It was then that the adorable six-year-old Rachel Yu appeared and insisted on being picked up by Uncle Alex. I obliged with a great mock heave and chatted to her for a couple of minutes. Mike Yu moved around issuing instructions in fast Chinese, then relieved me of his daughter and invited me in for breakfast. I politely declined and went off down the shaded alleyway before crossing the wide street of the Surrey village that I now called home, heading towards the convenience store. The traffic was calm as always through this attractive little hamlet, with a few friendly faces to nod at. Shop canopies were already down to combat the sun, tubs of multi-coloured flowers lining the road. A Family History bore had recently accosted me in the pub to tell me the village was over two hundred years old, and tried to kindle my interest in sepia photos hung on the walls showing proud shopkeepers posing in front of their premises and Victorian ladies taking a stroll along an even more deserted high street.

While waiting to pay for my milk, I could see back across the road to where Mrs Bannister, known as Mrs B, sat outside her pottery store. The ugly, old witch always had some terrible complaint or ailment to take up fifteen minutes. The husband had long since run away and the majority of the village were well beyond the polite sympathy stage. A number of people even suspected Mrs B of being behind a recent cowardly poison pen episode in the village. Next to Mrs B's was Betty Grable's hair salon, and then we had the Coffee Shop where the owner, named Marcus I believe, had a small problem with me, namely that on first arrival in the village I had met and promptly bedded his missus. If I had known of the man's existence at the time, I could understand and accept his lingering animosity. As I hadn't, he could go to hell and we would probably come to blows sooner or later.

Walking back across, I savoured a refreshing breeze picking up. The Red Lion was having its frontage hosed down by Mrs Lennox, empty kegs lined up ready for the delivery. Mike Yu stood at the public entrance of his Takeaway to hand me a bundle of mail.

'Thanks, Mike. Tell the lazy get I do have a letterbox, will you.'

I jogged upstairs, put the milk away, then went to the side of the doorway where I sat down on a thin black mat. I put on gloves and proceeded to throw a heavy rubber ball against the opposite wall. The ball thwacked into the gloves at different angles, my imagination keeping wicket at Lord's, the exercise giving me a stretch as well as getting my blood moving. Before getting too warm I stopped and prepared breakfast of eggs, toast and proper coffee. I sat in a springy chair, resting my cup on my pride and joy American pool table and looked through the door over the distant countryside. Beyond the railway line lay a patchwork of fields, some sprinkled with black plastic covered bails of hay, others glowing gold, one with tiny moving little dots of free-range chickens in front of white-washed farm buildings.

I scanned the letters. Bill, bill, bank statement, a postcard from Naples, bill. I dropped everything but the postcard.

I'll be back by now. Here's the postcard
you asked for. Love, Carla.

It made me smile. Back by now meant working together for the rest of the summer before she returned to study something or other at "Uni". She was nineteen years old and far too intelligent for me – just friends waiting for the right occasion to make the mistake of taking things further.

TWO

Ready for work, in my green dungarees and scuffed Timberland boots, I wandered around to the public side of the Takeaway, finding Mike Yu standing in conversation with an officious-looking man who was wearing a bad brown suit. I interrupted with the bare minimum of politeness.

'Mike, is this a good time to talk about the wasp infestation?'

Mike Yu smiled. 'This gentleman's insurance, Alex, not environmental health.'

'I thought I'd give it a try.'

'My friend, I promise you I'll sort it.'

I went to my car and drove off to work, making sure to notice the aggressive stare from Marcus at the Coffee Shop. It was a brief journey along winding lanes, the Audi superb, banks of green interspersed with flashes of beautiful countryside, before I pulled into the exclusive grounds of Kentmere Tennis Club where the drive forked into the main car park (Porsches, Mercs, etc) and the staff car park (Rovers, VW Camper van). On the outside tennis courts were the aimless wanderings and thrashings of the club members, then up the manicured lawn with its big *K* crafted out of pink geraniums to the space-age grey and silver main building itself, the yellow and white club flag portraying the original crossed racquets with the letters

KTC fluttered atop a flagpole. It all looked fairly quiet with the line of running machines sitting idle on the first floor and the pool deserted. Above the main entrance resided the members' bar with its sun terrace where two green waist-coated bar staff were setting up for the day. Neither of them were Miss Carla Jones, late of the city of Naples.

Before I could head in, I noticed a bare torso sprawled out on a hillock of parched grass, green dungarees rolled down his front. 'Oi!' I called, and the laidback Tim Marr turned his shaven head in my direction and smiled.

'All right, boss? I've saved a place for you.'

Tim was a handsome little fellow. If he didn't shave his head then he carried around a mop of loose black curls that made all females within a fifty mile radius want to mollycoddle him. I went across and joined him, easily imagining a line of about eight staff members relaxing under the cloudless sky. At the sound of tyres crunching in on the gravel, I briefly considered getting up in case it was management, the top man Mr Macro or his Draconian No.2, Brendan Tuohy, with his old Irish name. It was always fun watching his face curl up as it was mispronounced anywhere between Hungarian and Chinese. He was the only person I hated in the whole Kentmere Tennis Club, not counting the members.

I strained to see, and happily the car was on the rich side. It was a nice BMW 7-series. I recognised the driver as he stepped out, his white shirt very bright between black suit, name of Mathew Molina with his neat greying hair and aloof demeanour. He was something successful in fabrics, onto his second wife, the first drowned off

Majorca (accidentally, not by his hand); the new one was the infamous Tina Molina, a decade younger who he met while she was "working as a waitress in an Ilford cocktail bar". Raven-haired Tina always had a good bit of cleavage on show, whether dressed for a wedding or for the gym. Despite being more than occasionally dizzy, she was charming and funny and of course attractive, but with no career path or obvious talent beyond shopping, I was not surprised she appeared bored in the company of Molina.

The first time I set eyes on Tina Molina she was completely naked. It had been the previous Christmas and happened by pure chance; it could have been the humongous fifty-year-old Mrs Hardy in the buff, or that petite soap actress I only knew by her screen name. But when an excited Tim dragged me down to the staff changing rooms, where a bartender called John was to be found lying flat out on top of the lockers with his lunch and a full ashtray beside him, my puzzled enquiries were answered with Tim shushing me and John staring at me as if I'd committed high treason.

'The workmen who fitted the new air-conditioning,' whispered Tim, pointing at the silver piping overhead, 'sloppily left holes at the top of the wall. What's on the other side of that wall? The Ladies' changing room.'

I remembered the rush of guilty excitement. John, who that month received a written warning for being permanently missing from his post, very graciously came down for a stretch from his vigil to allow me a look. Gingerly, I climbed up and put my eyebrows over the messy opening. Tina Molina was the only person within view, naked and towelling down and apparently admiring herself in a mirror. Ten guilty seconds seemed to last ten minutes before I came down, pretended to be a giggly teenager with John and then made to leave. Tim frantically grabbed at my arms.

'Where are you going?' he asked. 'Carla's in the Jacuzzi right now. She'll be through soon.'

Tempted though I was, my conscience got the better of me and I went back to work. I didn't insist on Tim doing the same.

I had to smile as I could hear Tina Molina's car approaching. It was a purple TVR Chimaera, a noisy beast which she parked (in a fashion) near the BMW and, yes, with a strain of my neck muscles I could spot cleavage as she hoisted her bag from the passenger seat and followed her impatient husband, him calling back half in jest, 'Come on, stupid woman.'

I relaxed again, briefly, until another vehicle arrived. This was a black BMW X5 driven by a Ms Karen Hennessy who was certainly worth having a look at. She jumped out in pink gym wear that was a bit young for her but she had a great body. Even from that distance I could make out her beautifully manicured nails as they moved through troublesome strands of blonde hair. From our chats around the Kentmere grounds I knew Karen owned a Child Model/Acting agency in Central London and that she lived in a cottage in desirable Walton-on-Thames, an area I always remembered as my dad spent five years in Walton prison in Liverpool. I watched Karen berate her young son for some reason and also snap at the docile

French nanny with them.

'Would you?' asked Tim.

'I would.'

A shadow moved across me and I looked up to see Carla Jones smiling down. She had caught a bit of sun while in Naples and with her thick black hair encroaching on her delicate temples she resembled a Persian beauty. Her pierced bellybutton was on show between short denim skirt and pink tee-shirt and she made my day already.

Carla dropped down between us. Without looking, I began to caress her flat midriff, and when she fended me off I claimed her hand to my chest.

'How was Italy?'

'Oh, it was superb, Alex. Everything about it I just loved.'

'Who did you go with?'

'Two friends from Uni, Peter and Julia.'

'Oh, Uni.' I placed heavy emphasis on the "Uni" but she missed it. 'Are they a couple?'

'No, actually they're not. They're both gay.'

'Really?'

'Yeah.'

We watched a jetliner deface the sky.

'I bet Julia's hot.'

'Oh, totally. I was thinking of giving it a go with her myself.'

'You should definitely do that.'

'And I also thought we could double date one night.'

'Excuse me?'

'Alex, you could pretend to be with me until you got into it.'

'Get into what?'

'We'd all look normal.'

'What, with Dale Winton and a Russian shot putter?'

'You thought Julia was hot a moment ago.'

'Well, I've gone off her.'

I turned on my side to watch her belly go up and down, catching a flash of ribcage and finding it marvellous to be near her flesh.

'Anyway,' she said, breaking the spell, 'what happened to replies to my texts?'

'My phone was nicked.'

'I'll let you off, then. Because you were seeing that girl from Watford. What happened to her?'

'She just buggered off. Probably with my phone.'

I kissed her hand and released it, then stood and kicked Tim's boot. 'Is this a good time, Tim?'

'Ready when you are, Boss.'

We all dusted ourselves down and headed towards the staff entrance just to the left of the big glass frontage.

'See you later, Alex,' Carla said quite brusquely and went off on a tangent.

I wondered if there was something wrong with her before realising too late that Mr Tuohy was ahead, pointing out parts of the building to a new employee. Tuohy's ferret features and Hitleresque shiny black head of hair turned towards us. I expected some sly derogatory comment to the new barmaid, something on the lines of "ah, two of our grounds men. Take a good look, you might not see them very often", but all that was forthcoming was a nod.

Tim had not even seen the man. He led me into the rabbit warren of offices, storerooms and staff locker-rooms, passing the odd gym assistant to let onto, before we came out at the Groundsman's room with a view out over the rear lawns.

'So, Carla's back,' Tim said.

'Yeah, she looks well.'

'Too right, she gave me a semi just listening to her.'

We found the final member of my team standing outside in his dungarees and sun-bleached blue baseball cap, his boots lace-less like a man in police custody, his hand rubbing his greying goatee beard while his eyes scanned a space somewhere up the side of the building. I stopped and looked up into the same spot, then the man reappeared from his worried reverie and smiled at both of us.

'Morning, Alex. Hiya, Tim. I won't trouble you with what was concerning me just then.'

I smiled and put an arm around the shoulders of Nigel Williams, guiding him out of the way of a Member jogging by. Nigel was an old mother hen, nicknamed Nervo by the staff, a moniker that he took in good spirit. I liked the man a great deal and had tried not to get into the habit of calling him Nervo, but it became inevitable. Only when the mickey-taking stopped being light-hearted did I defend my friend in a most forceful manner. Part of me wanted to be Nervo with his passion for the environment and his loving close-knit family, although not with that particularly dull wife. Nervo was obsessive about recycling and unnecessary waste, nagging management and all other departments to improve. He was often incensed by the degenerate lifestyles of some of the rich people he moved amongst every day. The grounds of the tennis club were his own private garden and litter was collected before it hit the ground.

Normally the first thing to be done would be to brew up, but Nervo said General Manager Macro was stomping around in a strop, so we geared ourselves up to get some serious work done. Nervo and Tim made preparations to paint the north fence, gathering everything from the storerooms further along the side of the building. Nervo was in charge of the paint and utensils while Tim brought the refreshments and portable radio. Members were streaming in now and there was a buzz of noise from the pool and gymnasium, as well as the squeak of tennis shoes. Two stunning women in tight black sports gear came walking past. I watched from inside a storeroom while Nervo tried not to stare and Tim stood leaning back in his boots with his head cocked to one side. Both men were given the same attention as a couple of bollards or litter bins in the way. The women's conversation could be heard by then.

'Xenobia, darling, it really is lovely to see you again.'

'And the same with you, Tiff. We really must do lunch this week.'

'Of course. Call me tonight and we'll set a date. I heard you've got a new boyfriend.'

'Oh, darling, he's gorgeous. But we're having a little

trouble communicating because he doesn't speak English and I don't speak Spanish.'

Then they were gone, leaving Nervo and Tim to look at each other. Nervo started to pile equipment up his arms. 'He doesn't speak English and she doesn't speak Spanish. What an idiot.'

I started to giggle as I rooted around in the cupboard. Then I heard the unmistakable voice of Karen Hennessy say hello to Nervo and him replying with a hello that managed to say "but what possible reason could a magnificent female like you have in speaking to me?"

'Would I be right in assuming you're Nerdo?'

I laughed out loud at that.

'I... I have been known as that, yes, madam,' said Nervo in the painful quandary of wondering whether to correct her.

I watched Tim raise a hand as he was glanced at but his silent "Tim" was given a silent "whatever".

'I need help with something and I was told you would be the man to speak to.'

'Errm, yes. What can I do you... what can I do for you?'

Karen turned her back to Tim and took hold of Nervo's arm, which he quickly released. 'I need to speak to Alex Robateau. An urgent matter. He said you would be able to bring me into staff areas to find him.'

She was a consummate liar. I exited the cupboard. 'Hello, Ms Hennessy. Have you come to take me away from all this?'

'Well, my garden is a bit of a mess, Alex.'

'I meant I'm ready to start my acting career.'

'You're twenty years too late, but I'll make some phone calls.'

We both paused until Nervo and Tim decided to break off from the entertainment and move away.

'Been in the gym?' I asked.

'Yes, just a brief run-around. Friday's my tennis day. Do you play?'

'Tennis? No, I hate it. That and squash. Cricket's my game.'

'My son's into cricket, well, the Kwik version. I bet you're a fast bowler.'

I shook my head. 'Wicket-keeper.'

'Oh, wicket-keeper.'

She seemed to be a tad nervous in my presence, this confident woman whose fiery personality had persuaded two members to resign after arguments over booking times or suchlike. Perhaps I should give her a wide berth. The more likeable Nichola Duckinfield from the previous night was as risky as I should go, though Karen Hennessy was looking remarkably sexy. The image of making love to Karen there and then flashed into my mind. There was only one life to lead after all and the nearby tennis players might not object.

'Out!' came a shout from the courts.

I made the decision not to scorn any advance if it was forthcoming.

'Anyway, Alex, the reason I popped across, you remember me mentioning the Children's Charity I'm involved with, well they're having a wine and cheese evening. I wondered if you'd be free.' She let me politely mull it over for a second. 'Only kidding, Alex. But would you like to go for a drink?'

'Yeah, sure. I'd like that very much.'

'How about tonight?'

Tonight? I was still sore from Nichola Duckinfield.

'You're on.'

We made arrangements before I watched her jog off. I was then approached by another blonde. When I mentioned that the only person I hated at Kentmere was Brendan Tuohy, I was forgetting Bars Supervisor, Rachel Calderbank. The briefest first impression of her was always that she was healthily sexy, in her early twenties, her highlighted hair cut short for swimming and other activities. It was one of my regrets that I had once been drawn towards her, while now I could so obviously see her selfish, awful character written all over her face. She came up the path looking at my latest fraternisation with aloof disapproval, which was a bit rich having once boasted of a lesbian fling with a gym member.

'You, Alan!' she barked.

Bitch knew my name.

'Alex.'

'Whatever your name is. Mr Tuohy wants you to unblock a drain in the main bar.'

I considered saying I would plunge her fucking head down it, but all she got was a nod and she flounced off from where she had come. In spite of Rachel Calderbank, I headed to the bar straight away because I wanted to see Carla again, noticing as I left that our little staff scene had been observed by Mathew Molina on the courts.

Carla's eyes flashed to me as I walked into the bar, but we were barred from talking as the big boss Tommy Macro was sitting on a stool. I smiled at Carla before letting one of the barmen I didn't know explain the problem below a grid in the tiled floor, really listening to Macro feigning interest in someone's backhand. Macro had come from running health clubs in Leeds, Birmingham and somewhere slightly more interesting like San Francisco. I didn't know whether darkest Surrey appealed; I rarely spoke to the man. He was very Money, liking casinos and flash cars. He kept his forty-something frame fit in the gym and often played tennis, making sure to just lose to the members. He was a big man, but I was sure I could take him.

'Good to have you back, Carla,' I heard him say.

'Thank you, Mr Macro.'

'How long are you with us?'

'Until September.'

'What would it take to make you permanent?'

'An act of God.'

'Ah, a little beyond me.'

I stood over the problem of the blockage, almost scratching my head. There was a nice loop of Spanish guitar tunes playing and a strong glare came down from the sun terrace. Carla leant over the bar to serve a disabled customer, her paisley green waistcoat and white blouse separated from her black skirt, with Macro letching at her pure teenage waist.

'What are you studying at university?' he asked.

'Leisure and sports science.'

'So why don't you work in the gym when you're home?'

'Because I'm a lifeguard there as well. Not very sociable, all that shouting "pack it in!".'

'I can see you're a very sociable girl.'

'Yeah, that's me.'

I was almost ready to put Macro's head down the drain. He was a big man, but I *still* thought I could take him.

'I tell you what, Carla. When you've done your degree you can be my leisure manager until you decide what you want to do.'

'You've got a leisure manager.'

'She's leaving.'

Carla smiled and went off to serve new customers. Brendan Tuohy minced up to the bar, glanced at my inactivity, then spoke to Macro.

'I've just sacked Paul Blundell,' said Tuohy.

'Remind me, what did he do again?'

'Threatened to blow up Mr Greenwood's car.'

Amused, Macro finished his orange juice and strolled up to the sun terrace, doing more PR work on the way.

'I saw her first,' announced Nervo, at the end of the afternoon as I finished showering in the Groundsman's room. I smiled. 'I did,' continued Nervo. 'Tell him, Tim.'

Tim declined to comment, drinking coke with his bare feet up.

'What have you got that I haven't?' Nervo asked. I held up my fingers. 'So you've got ten years on me. Age isn't everything.'

'Bare fingers, mate. I haven't got Mrs Williams.'

'More's the pity.'

'Hey, man,' said Tim. 'Is this one married?'

I stopped doing my hair in the mirror, unable to give the correct answer. I shrugged my shoulders.

When I was dressed, in decent shirt and trousers from my locker, I bid them goodnight and headed out to the car-park, hearing Nervo calling down the corridor, 'I could have had a woman like that, if I had something about me.'

I met up with Karen Hennessy on the ground between the car parks. She intended to follow me home so I could lose the Audi for the evening. Before getting into my car I looked up to the sun terrace in the hope of seeing Carla. Instead I had, separately, Tommy Macro and Mathew Molina looking down on me.

Mike Yu's Takeaway was busy with early evening trade as we arrived, but even so Mike came out to have a look at Karen. After parking round the back I jogged out and climbed into the X5, with all its windows down. Mike Yu was waving. Karen half smiled back. As we drove off I showed Mike a v-sign, calling, 'Are these yours?'

She took me to an exclusive restaurant somewhere in London and I was quite happy to be unsure of my whereabouts. We spent a long time in the bar after the meal just chatting and flirting, once she patted away dots of perspiration on my brow and suggested a cold shower together.

'Can I ask you, Alex,' said Karen Hennessy, 'where do you hail from originally?'

'I'm a Manchester lad.'

'Oh, really? I've got relatives who live in Manchester.'
'Not in my neighbourhood, you haven't.'

I entered her again with her ankles on my shoulders and her hands gripping the iron bedstead. In the half-light I looked down at the shiny flesh of her stomach and her still pert breasts, the thought of plastic surgery crossing my mind. Sweat flowed from every pore in my head and I silently cursed Mike Yu and his wasp-infested premises. Still, better to be there than a stuck-up hotel with some two-faced harlot of a receptionist glancing at me out of the corner of her mascara as if I was some kind of rent boy.

Karen Hennessy was abandoned to this enjoyment. No doubt she had been surprised that I turned down her suggestion of a hotel room for my "dreadful" flat with an aroma of Chinese food. The missing shower curtain, broken tiles and a dead wasp were not exactly the scenario she had in mind, but she quickly adapted and accepted the price of having her bit of rough at last.

I calculated it was almost dawn. A good time had by all, and I still enjoyed kissing her freely-giving mouth and moving inside her, but fatigue was setting in and my mind was morphing her into a relative of Hannibal Lector skinning me to the bone.

'Alex, don't come again.'

I was unsure whether I could. I pushed harder, surely not deeper, her pupils rolled upwards out of view.

'Killjoy,' I said.

'Don't come again,' she begged.

Her hands moved to my backside in what transpired to

be a good yoga position, pulling me in yet further, gasping then moving, gasping then moving, then suddenly in one thrust she had rejected me. My thoughts had flashed back seven years to the only other time that had been done to me, by Confused Catholic of Congleton. Karen, however, was not stopping proceedings. She scrambled round to kneel before me, her hair bedraggled and her face drained. I used a towel to remove some perspiration. While temporarily blinded she surprised me by going down into my lap. Jesus Christ, I thought, what was she like twenty years ago? I caressed her taut back with its sheen of moisture down as far as the outward curve of her hips, then all the way back up to her hair, pulling gently and twisting to be able to view her actions. She had about three quarters of me inside with a mischievous curl of the lip. As she had said candidly earlier in the restaurant, this was the culmination of months of longing for her, of admiring me from a distance, catching the occasional bout of manual labour with tee-shirt discarded, snatching a few words here and there, forcing girlfriends who hate tennis to play tennis. Now it was done, and done very well indeed.

'Come now,' she mumbled.

THREE

A few days after the Karen Hennessy Experience, I awoke early, straight out of my favourite dream of making love to my ex girlfriend, Chloe of Manchester, explicit and clear as day, before it cruelly faded away from me and I was forced to accept cold reality. I dressed in only tracksuit bottoms and took my coffee out onto the stairwell with its two sun loungers. It was a dewy morning out over the fields, with the promise of heat again later. My neighbour in the next flat was a dumpy Primary school teacher called Miss Brocklebank, not to be confused with Rachel Calderbank from the tennis club (I had once imagined living next to that bitch). For the hour it took Miss Brocklebank (did her pupils call her Bottle Bank?) to get ready for work, cheery music had been playing, finishing with The Nolans and *I'm in the mood for dancing*. We exchanged cordial waves as she set off in her red Fiat Cinquecento with its ludicrous alloy wheels.

I leant on the railings and looked along the back of the shops, with rattling activity at Mrs B's and a lorry backing in at the Coffee Shop. The wife of Marcus came into view and for the life of me I could not remember her name. I could remember her curvy body that was in jeans and flowery top. She was in flip-flops and her hair was a mess, and it kind of summed up the sexy plainness about her. Kimberley, that was her name. I thought it best not to stare, watching instead in a sleepy fascination two airliners on an apparent collision course.

It was coming up for a year since the move from Manchester, officially traipsing after a girl but in truth desperately needing to change my environment. I had blagged my way to a job on a golf course when my only experience of working outdoors had been doing pensioners' gardens on Community Service. Not long after being there, one of the club members told me about the position at Kentmere. I showed up for the interview with Tommy Macro ready to pretend that I had worked on the grass courts at Didsbury in Manchester (having once heard that Andy Murray played a pre-Wimbledon tournament there) and then was surprised to find that the Kentmere courts were concrete outside and carpet inside. Basically, Macro saw that I was fit and strong and hired me within five minutes. I quickly learned the ropes from the head grounds man, then took over a month later when that man retired through ill health.

'Alex!'

I considered pretending not to have heard Mrs B calling from the rear of her pottery store.

'*Alex*,' she intensified the strain in her voice.

'Morning, Mrs B.'

'Have you got a minute, Alex?'

Her pained expression was working overtime. She really did put it on with a shovel. I placed down my cup and joined her.

'Oh, thank you, Alex.'

'How are you this morning, Mrs B?'

'I just need a new back. Will you put my shutter up for me? I can't manage it.'

'Of course.'

I obliged and she thanked me again.

'Okay, now, Mrs B?'

Her eczema encrusted hand went to my forearm in a preamble to unburden some trauma. Thankfully, Mike Yu made an appearance, allowing me to excuse myself and move swiftly away.

'Mike.'

'Hiya, Alex.'

'I don't want to bug you but I'm losing pounds every night.'

'Then stop using prostitutes.'

Mike Yu had a good giggle, liking that one.

'Pounds in weight, sweating in my airless tomb.'

'Don't worry. I've got someone booked to look at the wasps.'

'That's great.'

I set off up the stairs, until the racket of a scooter coming up the side of the Takeaway stopped us both. Under his orange helmet, Tim Marr gave us a lacklustre wave as he parked up.

'While I remember,' said Mike Yu, 'I've got more mail for you.'

'Is this postman taking the piss, or what?'

'No, no, this was a special courier. I'll get it for you.'

'Cheers, Mike. Give it to this guy, will you.'

A moment later Tim wandered into my flat, dropping a manila envelope onto the floor near the phone.

'Coffee?' I asked.
'Please, mate.'
'Beth?'
'Yep.'

We sprawled out in the lounge area with a music channel on the television. Tim lived in Hounslow with Nervo, rather, a few streets from Nervo while Tim shared the family home with his sister since their parents moved to Turkey. I thought of Beth, his seventeen-year-old girlfriend with the beautifully pure face and nubile body, and the personality of a just been fed terrier. Her nagging was infamous, constant, and occasionally she would fall completely off the logical deep end and go for Tim hell for leather. It would last for hours, his natural calmness only infuriating her more. Whenever she went even further by splitting up with him or actually attacking him, throwing punches like a boxer on one occasion, left, right, left, right, with Tim covering up, he always surfaced at my place for considered, mature analysis and advice.

'Fucking sack her this time, man.'

'I can't, she's a babe.'

'Listen, Tim. I know what you're saying, I've been there. But she's off her rocker. Get away and find someone normal.'

'This isn't what you usually say to me.'

'I know, because Beth's a babe. Christ, you're ageing me. Why can't you go round to Nervo's and talk to him. Better still, take her round there. They're made for each other.' Tim drifted to his feet and picked up a cue off the pool table, casually hitting balls around. 'If you rip the cloth I'll let her kill you.'

'Alex, what can I do? I love her.'

'Have you slept?'

'Together?'

'No, have you slept?'

'Do you think she'd let me sleep?'

'Well, go and have an hour in there. And don't complain about the perfume.'

'There you go, see. I should be dating much older women like you.'

'Excuse me? Have you seen any pensioners come out of here? I see sexy women at their sexual peak. Probably because I can't handle insane teenagers like Beth. Maybe you should see other people. If you love one another you'll come back together eventually.'

I threw on a top and stepped into my trainers.

'I'm going for a ride. I'll do something to eat when I get back. Okay?'

'Yeah. Listen, I know I won't be able to sleep. I'll prepare a fry-up while you're out.'

'Fine.'

I carried my black mountain bike down the stairs and set off round the Takeaway. I would do a lap of my regular circuit before it became too hot, starting off down the High Street, passing the garage and left up onto a canal towpath. Within minutes I was in glorious isolation, moving up the gears, the dirty brown canal empty apart from a family of ducks. I dived off briefly along a farm track before a new road climbed up through a wooded area. Overhanging trees lined the road to filter out light, dropping the temperature slightly. The road dipped out to a mini-roundabout and I was indifferent to the expensive cars flashing by on the dual-carriageway to the north east of my village. On for another mile, passing a farm and a local garden centre, then stopped for a while leaning against a stone bridge, breathing deeply, looking far along the hazy railway line. I allowed myself to be drawn out into the false tranquillity of the track, enjoying the quiet – such a change from my previous city-dwelling existence. I felt the sun for the first time, adding to my impressive tan that emphasised my health and fitness. I chose not to remember a time when I was pale and out of shape. I chose not to remember a lot of things.

I again allowed myself to visualise the pure skin of Tim's Beth, with her deep black eyes and always with her blonde hair scraped back into a ponytail. Because of my tennis connection at the moment, I often thought of Beth as a stunningly attractive version of the pretty former champion Martina Hingis. In the early days of knowing Tim, I had wanted to steal Beth away from him, especially as she clearly went in for the "new boy syndrome". Now she was like the wife of my younger brother. I decided it was wrong to be anything other than neutral with Tim's domestic situation. It was a natural progression to start off with a screamer.

Shaking the first inklings of arousal over Beth from my mind, I cycled on through a number of small villages, coming across holidaying kids on bikes and playing football, noting that the junior members at the club had been well-behaved that year, with only two fights and three acts of copulation on the courts. I came in from the other end of the village, making sure to spit on the road near the Coffee Shop and then freewheel past Mrs B in her usual seat and back around the side of the Takeaway. I took a long shower before putting on the news and taking a look at that manila envelope near the phone. On inspection, it seemed like a heavy duty tax form, which I could do without at that moment, and besides, Tim was there.

'Grub's up.'

'Nice one.'

The fry-up had turned into bacon sarnies and milk which we consumed outside.

'Are you mulling over my problems?' asked Tim, as I seemed to be deep in thought.

'No, I'm wondering what handicap you'd have to give me if I raced you to work on my bicycle.'

'I'd have to go via Southend.'

'Yeah, it's not a good idea, is it?'

'What I could do is go home for a couple of hours kip. That'll even things out.'

I took his plate. 'Come on, let's make a move. Nervo will be panicking about his break.'

I decided that I would cycle to Kentmere anyway. I locked the flat and trotted down to Tim starting the scooter. After four attempts Tim gestured for a push start.

'This would have been a good handicap!' I shouted into the helmet before pushing Tim and the scooter up the side alley, the engine still spluttering. Tim went for the whip and I got my legs pumping on the road past the Takeaway.

The scooter roared into life and off it went, Tim leaving me with a Royal wave.

And there she was, her blue eyes joined with mine, standing outside the pottery shop, wearing a purple sweat-top and grey jogging bottoms that flashed her achingly erotic midriff. Her light brown hair was parted in the middle and pulled into two long bunches down to her shoulders. She was early twenties with a delicate forehead and eyebrows that dropped catlike into a sharply defined button nose, and then those full lips with a suitably brazen covering of pink.

Mrs B was there encouraging her to go in and browse. I prayed that the hag would need me for something, but she just went in. The girl broke the stare and followed Mrs B inside, asking her a question about a type of vase. I just stood there in the road. Probably she just thought I was some moron pushing a scooter up the street. Maybe she thought I was a really handsome moron pushing a scooter up the street. Perhaps she was a stuck-up Hooray Henrietta who would have looked down her perfect nose at me if the moment had lasted longer than three seconds. Anyway, it was gone now, I told myself. You get one of those a lifetime. You should not even consider rushing upstairs to spy on her departure. I would simply allow her to uplift my soul for the rest of the day, and then I would get on with the important business of hating her with a vengeance. Surely something as angelic, controlled, as fresh as that had to be completely and utterly up herself. Get off the street, Alex.

'Alex.'

Mrs B had come back out. Mother of Satan, Mrs B had come back out.

'Mrs B?'

'I need another lift. The last time, I promise.'

I was finally off the road, trying to slow myself from running to help Mrs B, hearing her tell the girl that Alex would get the right box down. The beautiful perfume in the shop was definitely not Mrs B's brand. The girl had her back to me so her rear and lower back had to be inspected. She stood to the side to let me pass but said nothing, not a fucking word, not a "thanks", not a "there you go". I quickly decided she must be that aloof ice queen with the trust fund and the "Uni" knobhead boyfriend. What qualities would she see in me anyway? I was the scooter pusher and now I was the box fetcher. I accepted the thanks of Mrs B, wanting to glance at and memorise the girl's face and bare abdomen but missing both as I shuffled sideways and out the door.

I cycled the thirty minutes to Kentmere Tennis Club, chased all the way by a grey void of a thunderstorm that carried intoxicating electricity in the air. With the hairs on the back of my neck standing up, I thought about the girl all the way, rating her above every girl I'd ever had, or failed to have, above every girl I'd worked with, bought a sandwich from or glimpsed from a passing bus in Barcelona. But on arrival all the different aspects of her beauty had blurred with my maddening sense of longing and frustration and I wanted to start hating her early.

A heavy downpour scattered several tennis players

indoors as I arrived at Kentmere. Tim was in the office working on some signs to encourage members to kindly leave the car-park at less than 50mph.

'You got here, then,' I said. 'Has Nervo had his break?'

'He's on it now. Then he's going to fiddle with some lights in the gym, so he should be here soon asking for help.'

I sat down and went through some paperwork I could do on autopilot anyway. Tim made me a cup of tea. Soon Nervo was there seeking assistance which we duly obliged with, putting up with interference from Leisure Manager, Sue Stone. There was a story around the place that Macro had hired her after she passed his test; namely that she did not object to having her breasts interviewed first.

Beyond the joggers on the running machines, I could see the shower had passed, so on the way back to the office I went through the bar to check that the sun terrace was not slippery. I looked down over the grounds, hearing boisterous players back on the courts and watched a black and yellow helicopter cross the sky from east to west. It was still breezy up there with the club flag snapping above my head. Yes, she was still with me.

Two women in tracksuits disturbed my peace, looking for a dry place to have their sports drinks after being in the gym. The older one ignored me, and I noted with distaste the sunglasses with the blob of gold at the temples, but the younger one with the wild black hair gave me a smile.

'Hello, Alex.'

'Hello, Mrs Molina. Worked hard, I hope?'

'I'm effing knackered, Alex. And just call me Tina.'

Tina Molina always held herself with a devil may care manner, long since given up pretending that she belonged in the rich Surrey set, knowing they could all see an Essex council estate in her.

'Alex, why aren't you on the fitness staff so that you could give me a rubdown?'

'What's wrong, are they not up to the job down there?'

'Well, today, one of them's a lemon and the other's a lad who looks about twelve.'

I crossed my arms on my dungarees, intrigued as ever by this firebrand.

'May I make a suggestion?' I offered.

'Of course.'

'You should get a job here yourself. Then after a hard shift I'd be happy to ease your pains in the staff room. We're a friendly team here. Aren't we, Harry?'

4ft 11ins Harry Madox, in his oversized green waistcoat, was carrying up drinks for an elderly couple. 'Sorry?'

'I was just saying the staff room is a hotbed of passion.'

'Yeah, it's a regular Roman orgy every night. There you go, Mrs Rosen. You sit down here. It's been under the umbrella.' Harry took the opportunity to ogle the two women, his tray tucked under his arm. He shared a look with me, leaving with, 'That's... very, very cheeky.'

Tina Molina flirted with me a little while longer, once putting her hand on top of mine. 'Alex, it's been ages since I had an orgy. Perhaps we could sort something out with you and your team.'

'They're very shy boys, Tina.'

Harry's partner on the bar was Carla, who began milling about the sun terrace, half pulling a face which I noticed. Finally she butted in. 'Sorry, Alex, Mr Tuohy's looking for you.'

I excused myself from the two women and followed Carla down into the main Club bar.

'I thought I'd save you from being mauled,' she said.

'Thank you. She's all right, really.'

Two young bartenders were waiting for Carla. She acknowledged them with a wave and said to me, 'We're going to take a break outside. Do you want to come along?'

'What, and pretend I just want to be your work buddy when really I want to screw you very hard?'

She rolled her eyes at my sarcasm and left me with a smile and a pat on the chest.

'By the way,' I called, 'I'm out with Tim and Nervo on Friday. You're invited.'

'Good. It's a date.'

I needed a day off, my eyes were feeling like they belonged in a dead cod through lack of sleep and over exertion. I slept in until ten, had breakfast and cleaned the flat a little before settling in to watch the third Test Match between England and India. The last two weeks had been fairly hectic, what with the annual Kentmere tennis tournament followed by covering for Nervo's camping trip to Devon. At the same time I had been juggling the girl from Watford and the asylum seeker from Romania, then came

Nichola Duckinfield and Karen Hennessy.

There was a metallic rattling outside as England lost their fourth wicket to a stupidly rash shot outside the off stump. 'Double first at Cambridge, what a twat.' The racket out front caused me to go and look through the bedroom window. There was a man on a ladder with a white mask over his mouth and he was not the window cleaner.

'Don't mind me,' the man mumbled. 'Just dealing with the wasp problem.'

I politely nodded at him, then looked down for Mike Yu, but if he was there he was out of sight. I looked along the street. Damn, just missed the woman who walked as if pushing a wheelbarrow as she passed a silver Renault Megane with the rear off-side spare in place parked up outside the Red Lion. My sister loved the Megane's funny stick-out boot and was saving up for one. There was a black Citroen Saxo the other way near Mrs B's, with a beautiful girl getting out. As she turned and the wind blew her hair from her face, to my astonishment it was the same girl again, back at the pottery shop, this time in jeans and an unfortunate choice of blue and white striped Argentina football top that nevertheless hugged her body superbly. I threw the curtains shut on the strange man on the ladder. I estimated there was not enough time to wash and shave, just to change out of the tee-shirt with last night's tomato soup down it. The second top passed the smell test and I was downstairs entering the back of the Takeaway. Mrs Yu and a relative were sitting preparing some kind of foodstuff over buckets. Both of them smiled and ushered me through when I asked for Mike. I gave Rachel Yu a peck on the head before taking hold of Mike Yu's arm and leading him round his counter.

'*He's doing the wasps,*' protested Mike Yu. 'He's doing them.'

'That's great. I think we should consult over the standard of his work.'

We stepped out onto the pavement, Mike Yu a little bemused, especially as I made him stand on a certain spot.

'Alex, mate, what's happening?'

'Fit girl in Mrs B's.'

'How fit is she?'

'Beyond belief.'

'Oh, good.'

Mike Yu started pointing up at the roof. I kept an eye on Mrs B's doorway.

'Hopefully she'll be coming out soon.'

'Alex, do you find this pick-up technique usually works?'

'I'm not trying to pick her up. I just want to see her one more time before I die. Anyway, shut up, she's coming out.'

The girl came out looking our way. Mike Yu's acting style had him pointing at a passing satellite as he gawked at her. I was sure I detected a little knowing smile on those lips and felt so silly I started pointing as well for the hell of it. Paranoia kicked in, surely she had me down as a complete nutter by now. She was fiddling with her car keys, then she slowly got into the Citroen. I noted that there was no glance at herself in the mirror, no fine tuning of the hair. There had been no purchases either. Maybe she had ordered something that I could deliver for Mrs B. Perhaps she was related to Mrs B. That was too horrible to consider. She drove off in the opposite direction.

The man came down the ladder, clipped down his mask and started to fill out a form. 'All done, Mr Yu. Give it a couple of days before you remove the nest. Or you could leave it there. The wasps won't go in it again.'

'Wait a minute,' said Mike Yu. 'Back up a bit. You're not taking it away?'

'No, Mr Yu. We don't do that.'

'What kind of pest control is that?'

I smiled at Mike Yu, took a last look up the hill and then went back to the cricket.

FOUR

We all agreed on the West End for the night out, although Mrs Nervo was told we were staying local. That Friday, Carla's old Beetle managed to get us from Kentmere to my village. I glanced over my shoulder at Nervo as he was trying to speak to Carla above the gruff noise of the engine, while he looked on with horror at Tim, who had discarded his shoes and socks and was in the process of picking his bare feet.

'Recycling,' stated Tim, nibbling a tiny morsel of skin.

'You should stay with me and Ann,' Nervo told Carla. 'What would your mum say about staying with Alex?'

'I'll be fine,' she called back. 'He's promised to be a perfect gentleman.'

I haughtily showed agreement. 'I've changed the sheets,' I assured her, patting her thigh.

'She's met him, Nervo, anyway,' she told him.

'I bet she has,' said Tim.

Carla smiled at him in the mirror. 'Hey you, don't cast aspersions at my mother.'

We dipped past the church into the village which was fairly quiet except for the pavement outside the Red Lion where the clientele were dealing with the warm evening. As Carla came to a stop, a body came flying backwards out of Mike Yu's Takeaway as if it were a Wild West saloon.

'Oh, no,' said Nervo. 'What's going on here?'

The ejected youth got to his feet and joined a friend in a scuffle with a ranting Mike Yu in the doorway. Tim and I left Nervo with Carla and approached as the two men were pushed into the street. I acted all conciliatory, with hands up, calling, 'Eh, lads, what's the trouble?'

Mike Yu stopped talking at a hundred miles an hour and seemed quite happy to have me there, plus the two youths appeared willing to have a calming third party bring a way out of the commotion, but then Tim came in and slammed one of the men up against the glass frontage, prompting an exchange of punches until I managed to part them. I was surprised at my usually languid friend being so aggressive.

'What's rattled your cage?' I asked him.

The two youths decided to depart the scene, firing expletives off at Mike Yu. I let go of Tim's shirt, seeing that his expression was still as vague as always, and turned to see Mike Yu already back to his happy self. Carla was there with an arm protectively around my waist, which I found very endearing and held her back.

'Gives a bit of colour to the day,' Mike Yu was saying. 'Well, hello, who are you?' he asked of Carla.

I introduced them, 'Carla, Terry-Thomas. Terry-Thomas, Carla.'

Nervo tried to put an arm around Tim but was swiftly rebuffed. Carla gave Tim a slap on the arm.

'What are you doing fighting?' she scolded him. 'I'm going to tell Beth on you.'

'I pretended he *was* Beth.'

She checked his face, with a little bump coming up on

his left cheekbone. I asked for her car keys to put the Beetle around the back for the night. There was a taxi already on order, so Carla swapped embraces with Nervo while we waited.

I jogged back out front to see Tim playing with his phone.

'Boasting about your fight?' I asked.

'No, checking the snooker score. It's four-all.'

'Remind me, why bet on Higgins?'

'Because I want Stevens to win. I fucking hate Higgins, but he's playing so well. This way I can't lose.'

'You can't lose if you don't bet. What do you win, anyway?'

'A tonne. That's why I'm nervous. But it's like waiting for Spurs to concede a goal.'

I smiled and looked around, catching sight of Kimberley at the Coffee Shop staring at me while she waited for customers to seat themselves. Our eyes locked until she had to take an order.

Heavy cloud cover brought on a premature dusk, adding to the clammy feel of the evening. Beth was there outside the bar which was the agreed meeting place, looking striking in an all white outfit, going for Tim straight away for keeping her waiting. He looked away with a hound dog expression, before she saw his swollen cheek and changed into the perfect concerned girlfriend. Loving the attention, he shrugged it off as nothing, and said he might tell her about it later. Beth hugged and kissed Carla, not bothering to introduce the sullen girlfriend she had with her who was immersed in texting on her phone.

'Hiya, Alex,' smiled Beth.

She could be lovely when she wanted, if only she could lose the petulant streak. I smiled back at her.

The buzz inside the bar suddenly burst out when the door opened, swallowing us in manic dance music. Nervo showed remarkably agile moves which had us all laughing. I grabbed my friend as we all went in. We managed to be served and squeezed out a place, talking close to each other's heads.

'My ears will be ringing all night,' a back to form Nervo said to me.

'I love this heavy beat. You can feel it coming up through your shoes.'

I watched Carla laughing with a lad she knew from somewhere. Red and yellow lights flashed across her face. When she touched the man's arm to lean closer I noticed her long feminine fingers, and her bare lower back had great toning, from all her horse riding, no doubt. I watched Tim and Beth in a comfortable embrace, and next to them I smiled as Beth's friend continued to tap into her phone. Carla became free, so I moved across to hold her from behind.

'Carla, how long before we blow these jokers and go somewhere else?'

'*Blow these jokers*?' she laughed. 'I can't "blow these jokers" because I've just pulled.'

'What, with that lad?'

'Yeah, I'll be staying at his, by the way.'

'I'm afraid I can't allow that. You're my responsibility

tonight. What would I say to your mother?'

'Now, then, not jealous, are we, Alex?'

'Possibly.'

I pointed to Beth's morose friend. 'Glad she could make it.'

Carla laughed happily.

After an hour we moved to a different bar, with Nervo leading the way, complaining to me and Carla about damage to his ear drums. Tim and Beth followed, quite inseparable, with Beth's friend trudging up the rear. I forged the way to the bar, holding onto Carla's hand. She stopped me to point out two men surrounded by a posse of girls. They were moderately famous West Ham United players.

'There you go,' I said to her ear, 'a career move for you.'

I took a good look around the room, spotting a group of forty something men trying it on with bored teenage girls. Nearby was the boisterous chanting of some kind of sports team. Beyond them, I spotted the real trouble, moving through the drinkers like sharks. Three youths with gold chains outside designer gear came strutting through, practising their only hobby of trying to look hard. I instinctively reached for Carla as they came by, one of them rudely putting a hand on Nervo's chest. Nervo watched them go with wide eyes before resuming a conversation with Beth. Carla had sensed my slight tension.

'What's wrong?' she asked below the pumping music.

'Nothing. Same again?'

'Please.'

I felt the warm skin of her waist and her hip pressed into my thigh. Her cheeks were a little flushed and close up to me her mouth was fresh and sensual. In fact, her presence was making me a touch horny. Probably for the best I managed to be served.

The evening flew by, our group joined periodically by various friends of Tim and Beth. Nervo gradually became inebriated as always, and this was probably why he was not allowed to go far from home. Through my own swimming consciousness I realised I had shared almost the entire evening solely with Carla, as if we were a couple. I had to smile to myself at the thought that strangers might think that. We had laughed together, chatted intimately, poked fun at Nervo and congratulated Tim on surviving the night without a domestic.

Buffeted by a passing gaggle of girls, Carla slipped her hand into my back pocket to steady herself. I kissed her forehead, then from her eyes I seemed to get the impression she was intoxicated not only from liquor but perhaps from the heat between our skin, mixed with my aftershave or my animal... she pinched me as I was smiling again.

'What are you doing?' she asked, giggling.

'It's good to have you home,' I told her.

Nervo poked his head in and smiled.

'I'm going now. My curfew, you know.'

'Are we moving on?' I asked Carla.

'Shall we call it a night?'

'If you like.'

'I'll get a taxi,' Nervo offered, then went outside.

Before saying goodnight, Carla had to gossip with Beth for a while longer. I smiled at Tim, putting an arm around him, indicating Beth.

'She's a darling,' I told him. 'You must be the problem.'

A happy Tim agreed. I looked between the bobbing heads of the customers, watching Nervo attempt to flag down a taxi. The synthesised beat in the bar cranked up to madness, matching perfectly with Nervo flailing and dancing about. A black cab seemed to have stopped. I tugged gently at Carla, slapped hands with Tim, kissed and hugged the fantastically nubile Beth, and even waved at her sullen friend. I glanced to check on Nervo's success, focussing just as a head-butt landed on my friend's face. My view was obscured, did I really see that? I pushed through a group of men, straining to see. The cab moved off, Nervo trying to lash out at three figures but then he just fell, out of sight. I moved at pace now for the door, pushing people out of the way, taking split-second glances through the front window, the beat filling my head along with adrenalin. Nearing the door I could see Nervo lying like a shop window dummy, his head being stamped into the pavement. Out onto the street I went, quickly followed by Tim, one Doorman stepping after us. The night air almost took my legs from under me. My ears exploded in buzzing and I might or might not have screamed over the street. I got to the prostrate Nervo, his left arm up in the air in an unconscious cry for mercy, and started throwing great haymaker punches. Three more youths came in from the side as Tim arrived to take them on, punching in his own mad staccato style but they were on him like dogs, dragging him down. Tim was overpowered, held firmly, one of the youths kicking rhythmically up into his face with the style of a Can-Can dancer. I landed two cracking punches and my main attacker backed off. It was all happening in a blur, so at first I could not comprehend that Tim was close to having his nose bitten off. I responded to the horrific act with three blows to the back of the biter's head, freeing Tim whose face was now a mask of blood. I felt a punch that seemed to want to snap my spine, then another punch came around to the side of my jaw. I swung about with a roundhouse martial arts fist that sprayed blood and mucus across the street, then suddenly the gang bolted away down an alleyway.

Tim was down on his knees in a right mess, while at first I was not in any pain, feeling only of chewing gum for twenty-four hours. I could see Tim's face swelling, a big damaged tomato. I tried to help him up.

'I'm okay, Alex. I'll just stay here a minute.'

Two large nursey type women were there tending to Nervo as a crowd gathered. Carla and Beth pushed their way through, both going to their respective men. I felt Carla next to me as we watched Nervo being cared for, his head caked in blood and grime, one of the women cosseting him in her hands while the other phoned for an ambulance. Tim was up now. He could take it as well as dish it out, and he tried to smile at Beth through his blood, but I really wanted to cry. I was shocked too, not at the unsolicited street barney but the stamping and the biting. I shivered at the image of that animal hanging off Tim's face. Now pain screamed out from my left arm, where on inspection I found a deep gash through my upper arm and my shirt shredded. It was a clean cut and I was surprised to see there was no blood coming from the gaping wound. Through the sound of sirens on the nearby roads I was aware of Carla saying something into my ear.

The gay, balding, Scottish triage nurse was not exactly mortified with the injuries to Tim's face, giving him a bandage to press on and a five hour wait. At first I declined to be looked at but the nurse spotted my cut arm and said it would need stapling. So we sat amongst our fellow Friday night casualties with Carla and Beth waiting for news on Nervo and for his wife Ann to arrive. After an hour of motley people watching, both in the flesh and on Jerry Springer high on the wall-mounted TV, I stood with a big groan, pain in my mouth, arm and hands. My lower back seemed to be made of iron. I went for a slow wander. The triage nurse currently had a large woman in a distressed state, crying out for her "Dennis! Dennis!" and refusing to stop lolling out of wheelchair provided. I read all the information on all the walls. A model in a particular Drink Drive poster reminded me of the girl from Mrs B's shop. I huffed and turned away as Ann Williams and a woman friend hurried in to the care of Carla and Beth before being taken to the nursing staff. I eased myself back down next to Tim, blood dried black on his elephant face. Nevertheless, Tim was sat cross-legged and cheekily looking at me. He said as if with a heavy cold, 'Higgins lost.' We both had a good laugh.

Nervo had regained consciousness in the ambulance and been talking with doctors while they worked on him. He was scanned and x-rayed, thought to have just heavy bruising and dental damage, but would be kept in overnight for observation and more tests. Ann Williams reported back to a patched up Tim and me that he seemed to be all right and promised to call us later, insisting that we should not wait around the hospital any more.

The taxi quickly dropped Tim and Beth before going off into the black countryside, a quiet Carla curled up child-like onto my chest. I felt the movement of her breathing against me as I stared up to a marvellous display of stars, something which I had come to cherish with many hours spent sitting outside my flat. The taxi driver never said a word as he got us home and after he had u-turned and driven away there was the buzz of silence on the street. She was shivering against me even though it was a mild night.

'Are you all right?' I asked her.

'Not really.'

'Let me look after you.'

'It should be me looking after you.'

'Now, come on, don't be silly.'

I stroked her hair and cupped her face. She tried to smile at me.

'Carla, I think you're lovely.'

'You'll have me blushing in a minute.'

'Come on, let's go up and eat something.'

We went into the black alleyway arm in arm. I stopped her halfway and put my hands around her waist. As I closed the gap between us I sensed her breathing falter. My lips made gentle contact with her left ear.

'There's something very important I have to tell you.'

'What?' she replied in slight panic.

She slipped her hands inside my shirt to hold my body. I playacted a wince from my bruising and we both giggled.

'I don't know how to tell you this.'

'Alex, you're scaring me. Tell me.'

'Okay.' I paused. 'I don't think I can carry you over the threshold.'

She hit me on the shoulder and I gasped for real, and she was instantly apologetic, then we laughed and helped each other to the flat.

She perused my CD collection while I went for a wash. My suggestion of James Blunt fell on deaf ears. She chose some Adele. I put on a vest, checking the pad on my cut arm as I rejoined her.

'Alex, can I get changed? I think it's Tim's blood on me.'

'Of course. Through there. Put on anything except my basque.'

'Ooh, saucy.'

I put the grill on while she was changing, calling, 'Crumpets.' I knew she wouldn't go rooting, she was back out quickly in cotton trackie bottoms and a purple sweat top previously owned by my heartbreaker ex-girlfriend Chloe, left behind in our Manchester flat with the cat and no furniture. I watched Carla perusing a magazine, the purple top leading me into melancholic thoughts, but then Carla girlishly skipped across to accept her crumpets and sat cross-legged next to me on the sofa. I watched her eat for a minute.

'What?' she finally asked.

'You can't beat a good crumpet, can you?'

She cracked up laughing and then crying as the stressful night took its toll. I laughed gently and took her hand from her eyes, accepting her into a hug. 'Carla, baby, it's okay.'

'Alex, don't let go.'

'I won't.'

We stayed close for the rest of the early hours, watching the music channels and then the film *Love Actually* which I thought would be rubbish but turned out to be surprisingly good. Our legs were either next to or across each other and finally she was lying flat out with her head on a pillow on my lap, me stroking her hair and sleep trying to engulf her. My fingers traversed her profile, as her eyes flicked up to my face. I touched the taut tendons in her neck, then her collarbones and lingered on the top of her chest below the baggy sweatshirt. My Ex, Chloe, used to sit with her knees inside it in a very cute protective manner and that was why it was so stretched.

'Why did they do that to Nervo?'

'Who knows?'

'So unnecessary, violence.'

'Don't think about it.'

She watched my hand slowly moving her skin as her chest rose and fell. She touched my face where it seemed to be a little swollen. 'You should have put some ice on that.'

'Nah. Well, yeah, I probably should. It doesn't matter now. Hey, we should sleep. Ann might ring in a few hours.'

'You're right. I'll be fine here, Alex. You go to bed.'

'Don't be silly. No, don't even start that. Come on, young lady, bed.'

'I thought you'd never ask.'

Her mouth dropped open slightly as she wondered whether she should have said that. I brought my fingers up to her lips. For a second she started to taste them and take them inside, before jumping up onto her knees.

'Odd friendship,' she said.

I was agreeing when the phone shocked us both.

'I didn't expect her to call at this time,' I said. 'Can you get it?' She glanced at the pillow on my lap. 'My back's seized up.'

She answered the phone, then waved it around as the caller hung up.

'Maybe it was your mum,' I suggested as she came back to stand in front of me. 'What were you saying about odd friendships?'

'You know, Alex, when we got out of the taxi I was thinking, "well, here at last. A little later than planned, my face a mess from crying, Nervo in hospital, you and Tim battered. Should I just ask you to share a bed? Or should I just join you wherever you ended up in the flat?" '

My hands held the back of her legs. She pulled my head to her stomach, with me groaning all the way.

'Stop it,' she laughed. 'Would you like a massage?'

'Under normal circumstances that would be a yes. I

don't think I'd feel anything. Can I massage you?'

'Under normal circumstances that would be a no. Give me a few minutes to get ready.'

She left me, to lock up and check the phone to discover that the caller had withheld their number. When I joined her in the bedroom she had discarded the tracksuit bottoms and was putting her hair up into a ponytail. I brought massage oil from the cupboard.

'You're joking?' she said. 'You've got oil?'

'You'll like this. It's what Tuohy puts on his hair.'

She laughed as she got on the bed, sitting back on her heels awaiting instructions. My vest was removed carefully, checking the plaster again. I moved in behind her, ridiculously nervous and excited at the same time, unsure as to how to proceed or of knowing exactly what I wanted to achieve, only enjoying it all immensely. I nuzzled into the fluff at the nape of her neck, touching under the hem of the sweatshirt to find no other fabric, just the tightness of her skin where hips met legs.

'Carla, turn around.'

She obliged and after minor prompting she removed the sweatshirt. I almost gasped, overjoyed on two counts, firstly that my friend was happily naked before me and second that she had just the most perfect breasts, full but not too big, and the circles around the nipples that for the life of me I could not find the correct name were large just as I liked. I had always believed that Carla had a beautiful body and now there it was held shyly but not shielded at all by her arms. There was nothing shy as she spun to lie on her front, inadvertently flashing everything to me and I was surprised at being shocked. She was clearly as excited as I was. I straddled her waist, determined to concentrate on providing a sensual massage, finding her body supple, taking my time and exacting force into her muscles.

'Where's the oil?' she asked after a sigh of pleasure.

'That was really shampoo.'

'This is wonderful anyway.'

Carla's face lifted and turned, showing an expression of guilty pleasure as well as confusion.

'What are you thinking?' I asked.

'Naked... Alex Robateau's bed... Naked.'

I was equally mixed up, fully aroused but guilt-ridden, struggling along. I could not think straight or decide what to do. I could still be massaging her back when the sun came up. Suddenly she turned over fully, tearful, pulling me down into an embrace.

'I don't know what to say, Carla.'

'Don't say anything.'

I kissed her lips with soft pecks.

'Alex.'

'Mmm?'

'I don't want to have sex.'

'Neither do I.'

I leant forward to switch off the light, leaving us illuminated only from the living-room, then lifted her legs and brought the thin covers over us and we snuggled in together.

'Do you really not want to?' she asked. 'Because I will if you want to.'

'I just want exactly this.'

'So we'll keep kissing?'

'That's the idea.'

'Are you keeping your pants on?'

'Too freaking right.'

'Okay.'

We found common ground to stay there entwined like that. Kissing ebbed and flowed through passionate to friendly, only occasionally I touched her bottom or allowed even the hint of an intimate caress elsewhere. Finally she succumbed to sleep and once again I found myself aware of dawn breaking.

FIVE

'What a bastard he is!'

Livid, I shouted it down the phone, walking to my bedroom with the handset to my ear, Tim on the other end. After checking each other's wellbeing and concurring that there was no further news on Nervo, he had just recounted a sick-leave call put into Brendan Tuohy, where the Irishman had said something along the lines of "are your injuries really severe enough to stay off?" and shown no concern at all for Nervo.

I was already up when the phone rang, having checked the bruising on my back and had a good stretch to loosen it up. I also possessed a banging headache from lack of sleep and my cut arm now screamed at me. I looked in on my guest, sprawled across the bed, making a toga out of the sheet. She rolled and said something unintelligible, but remained well away. Watching the girl's gentle breathing calmed me down a little. Tim asked how she was.

'She's fine. Still asleep. We'll talk later. Okay, mate. 'Bye.'

I clicked off the phone, chewing the antenna. I was just straining to move off to make coffee when her eyes started to open. I smiled at her and she pushed hair off her face.

'Alex.'

'Good morning.'

A tear flashed down her cheek.

'Hey, hey,' I said, getting to her as she began crying. 'What's up?'

'I've spoilt everything. I've ruined things with you.'

She held onto me.

'That's not true,' I whispered. 'Nothing's spoiled. Come on.'

She tried to stop crying.

'Alex, do you promise?'

'Of course.'

'God, how stupid am I? Acting like a child here.'

I held her, pulling up the sheet to cover her cleavage.

'It's early, Carla. Why don't you go back to sleep? It's been a heavy night.'

She lay back down, concerned about her appearance.

'You're beautiful,' I assured her.

I found her vulnerability captivating, her sweet demeanour taking my mind off my discomfort and headache. It was so tempting to get back into bed with her, just to have the joy of being so close again. I smiled as she actually gestured for me to join her, replaying in my mind her "because I will if you want to". Instead, I kissed her forehead and stood slowly up.

'I'll just be out here.'

I went through and got the coffee on, then silently swore inside the fridge at having no milk. Maybe a walk to the shop would be good for my back.

I put on my mules and a cap to stop the sun adding to the malaise in my brain. At the door, I spotted that manila envelope again, which I grabbed to have it done with.

There was just my name on the front with no address. It ripped easily, my fingers revealing a wedge of £50 notes in an elastic band together with a folded letter. 'Fuck...me.' I closed the envelope. I stood there puzzled, looking around the flat. Then I rammed it down into one of the pockets of my pool table and went out onto the stairs, my head banging even more now. There was no way I could deal with that right then. But the slow hobble down the stairs allowed me to think. There was nobody in the world who owed me money. It was inconceivable that somebody who had crossed me in the past would have an attack of conscience and make amends. The money could only be a bad thing. But what if it was a gift from someone like Nichola Duckinfield? That was out of order, yet it calmed the adrenalin running through my body. Ignore it for today, I ordered myself. Care for Carla, check on Nervo, rest.

Mike Yu was mopping the floor of the Takeaway as I looked in. There came an inspection of my bruised face and the bandaged arm.

'One hell of a night, Mike.'

'So I can see.'

'Mike,' I had to ask. 'That envelope the other day. Did you know the guy who delivered it?'

'No, Alex, I didn't.'

'Oh, right. Never mind. I just wondered.'

'Everything all right?'

'Yeah, fine, Mike. Off to the shops. Catch you later.'

I stepped into the street, straight into the path of the girl from Mrs B's, causing shared oomphs and apologies and steadying hands, then she smiled as she knew I recognised her. For just the briefest of moments I allowed myself to blatantly wallow in her presence, so close I could smell her perfume, sense all of her, though my muddled brain started struggling to take in every single aspect of her beauty and my eyes flitted around her face. I believed she was in denim, with jeans hanging low on her hips. There were purple-tinted shades on top of her head. She was looking at my facial injuries and tenderly reaching up without touching.

'Have you been fighting?'

There was genuine friendly concern in the question, as if she knew me. As I formed an answer I was strangely fascinated by just the sexiest mouth and freshest tongue ever.

'Just a little scuffle.'

'Oh.'

There came a little pause, where we both knew we should really say something. Then the woman who walked as if pushing an imaginary wheelbarrow steamed straight through between us. I did a comedy double-take after her.

'I'm Joely, by the way.'

'Alex.'

'I know. The lady in the shop said your name.'

I found I was swaying on my feet, the morning sun right on my face despite the peak of the cap tilted down. Feeling the prickly beginnings of sweat forming on my brow, I tried not to squint at her, desperate to appear cool but cursing the timing of this. I tried to find something to say that was not just a compliment, but then again why should I be worried, I had not sought her out. This was the worst possible time and then a nerve in my lower back chose to start shaking.

'Having trouble finding what you want?' I finally asked. 'Next door.'

'Well, that's the thing, you see. I was wondering how many times I have to come back to that terrible shop before you ask me out?'

It was said with a great sense of honesty, finishing with an almost apologetic expression, not like the kind of brazen come-on I had heard so many times before. In fact, I had never been spoken to in that manner. She obviously did not put herself on the line like that very much, if at all. Adrenalin banged through my chest once again and seemed to target my wobbling thighs. I was rarely thrown by anything, always fairly sure I had a handle on things, yet that morning I was gone. I was shocked by my fragile state.

'A couple more times should do it,' I heard myself say.

She remained composed, just the tiniest of baulks away from such a cruel putdown. My head was pumping my eyes from their sockets and I needed to lie down. Why I had said that I would never know, when I was fully aware of how special she was. Maybe she was just too nice. Maybe I felt undeserving to have her in my life.

'That's clear, then,' she said, without attitude, backing away and turning on her heels to her car. I closed my eyes, hating myself, wanting to go after her but also pleased somewhere deep inside to have retained my power in some perverse way. I watched her drive away, then forgot the milk and headed back to my flat.

'That told her,' I reflected on the way. 'You odd dickhead.'

I went upstairs, stared with fury at the pool table on the way to the bedroom, then stripped off and climbed into bed with Carla, tenderly holding her and disturbing her snoozing.

'Hello, you,' she said.

The little Indian batsman let a ball go through to the keeper.

'He didn't even try to hit that,' pointed out Carla, a little aggrieved.

I smiled at her, with her bare feet up on the sofa, wearing more of my clothes, looking more her happy self. Going back to bed had seen off the headache, plus my body had calmed down and was starting to feel less abused.

'Have you moved in?' I teased.

'Would you like that?' she threw back at me.

'I might do.'

Tim had called again with positive news concerning Nervo, and arrangements were made to go up to the hospital that afternoon. Carla had stayed for breakfast and we sat outside listening to some Bee Gees coming from next door before watching the start of the third day of the cricket.

I sat there and watched her, myself relaxed, feeling as if I had come through an emotional storm, with the night before having seen our friendship tested by violence, followed by fear and concern. I had held onto Carla until it had all gone away, then there had come the rejection of the girl from Mrs B's; Joely, Miss J. That would teach her for assuming her perfection could bring anyone she desired. For thinking Alex Robateau could be the flavour of the month. I was shaking my head; Alex Robateau was often flavour of the month.

I considered Joely to be an unusual name. In time I trusted that I would be able to blur the picture of her face and body, but unfortunately the name would haunt me. I was still struggling to understand why I had dismissed her like that. Why did I want to convince myself that she was so fake? What was wrong with telling her about Nervo in hospital and Carla upset and my back killing me? Take her number and call some other time. Very strange, Alex.

'Stop me washing up, then,' said Carla, standing.

'Yes, don't you dare wash up. You're my guest.'

'Thanks, Alex. I'd better go. One of us should do some work today.'

'Give Tuohy my love.'

'Make sure you give Nervo mine.'

She gathered up her blood-speckled clothes and found her car keys.

'That's me done. I travel light, you know. I'll get your clothes back to you.'

I gestured a "whatever" and stood to hold her. 'Come here. It was lovely being with you.'

'I don't want to go now,' she said into my chest.

'Then don't.'

She dragged herself away after pecks on cheeks and I

followed her out, leaning on the railings as she skipped downstairs.

'I'll see you soon, Alex.'

'Look forward to it.'

She drove away. I stayed there in the shade looking out to the west where a bank of dramatic nimbus or whatever clouds were building up.

I waited for the cricket lunch break before tidying myself up for visiting hour with Nervo, intending to pick up a sandwich from the bakery first. Exiting the alleyway, I could not help but look for Joely. If she was there, she was even more mixed up than I was, or she was back with her brothers. Instead I saw Karen Hennessy's BMW pulling up, with plain nanny and child sharing the passenger seat. Karen jumped out and we exchanged friendly kisses.

'I thought I'd just stop by to check you were all right,' she said.

'Thanks, I'm fine. Surprised you found the place again.'

There was just the briefest of hesitation before she noticed my bandaged arm. 'You've been cut?'

'What, this?' I let her half inspect it. 'I've had your name tattooed.'

'Very funny. What are you up to?'

'I'm going to grab a butty, then I'm off to see my mate in hospital.'

'Oh, Nerdo?'

'That's the fella.'

We walked together to the bakery and I enquired about the boy.

'My son, Cameron.'

I ordered a roast beef barmcake from Sullen Sally in the hairnet and Karen decided to pick up a couple of iced doughnuts.

'Not for me, you understand. For Cameron.'

'Sure. How's business?'

Her facelift dropped. Sullen Sally asked about mustard and I nodded at her.

'I'm not happy there any more,' said Karen.

'Oh?'

'I might move on.'

There was a bib from a car horn. Tim sat there in a rusty light blue Mini.

'Your lift?' asked Karen.

'Unfortunately it looks like it.'

'Well, I'll leave you to it. I hope Nerdo is okay.'

I laughed and kissed her, taking in her expensive perfume and the warmth of her skin. 'I'll give him your regards. Thanks for coming round – sorry it was a wasted journey, Karen.'

'No, it's not been wasted. Can we meet up again?'

'Yeah, sure. I'll call you.'

'You promise? Maybe we can do lunch?'

'Definitely.'

I watched her go while my sandwich was literally thrown together by Sullen Sally. I paid and started to eat immediately as I slowly stepped out to assess the transport. 'What... the fuck... is that?'

'It's Beth's. Come on, get in. Nervo's home.'

'They let him out? Couldn't they have sectioned him

while they had him in?'

The Mini struggled towards Hounslow. I fiddled with the wobbly dashboard while Tim played with the stitches in his nose.

'Is your back all right?' he asked me.

'Yes, mate.'

'So you're up for cricket practice tomorrow?'

'Of course.' Part of the dashboard fell onto my lap. 'But I'll pick you up, right?'

Ann Williams stood chatting with a neighbour at the door when we arrived so we just smiled at her and walked through to the lounge where Nervo was propped up on the sofa bed in his pyjamas. I laughed straight away.

'Oh, cheers,' said Nervo.

His head was swathed in bandages with brown tape at the ears, his eyes were black and his bottom lip ballooned out as if he were a member of some Amazonian rainforest tribe. He pointed at the lip as if to ward off any Sting jokes.

Tim went straight for the grapes and the TV remote control. I sat down next to the bed to enquire of my friend's health. The only thing concerning Nervo was being off work.

'No worries there, mate,' I told him. 'Tuohy, bless him, says to take as long as you need.'

'Are you sure?'

'Of course.'

Tim found the cricket and settled himself in, despite Nervo's protests. He was having some trouble speaking but I was pleasantly surprised that he seemed to be taking it so well; helped it turned out that he had no recollection of the night whatsoever.

'Well, that's good,' I said. 'Apart from forgetting the stewardess you met.'

'He'd better not,' said Mrs Nervo, coming in with tea and biscuits. 'Has he told you what a difficult patient he is, Alex?'

'I can imagine, Ann.'

She left us to it. Tim was up for the drink.

'This is better than being at home.'

'Did you have to bring him?' Nervo asked me.

'He brought me, in Beth's Mini.'

'That death trap? Beth, and Carla, both phoned to see how I am. More than you buggers did.'

'We're here, aren't we?' stated Tim, settling back down in front of the television.

'Well?' Nervo asked me. 'What happened with Carla?'

'I thought you had no memory?'

'Bits are coming back to me. Well?'

'Well, what? Nothing happened.'

'She's well into you, sunshine.'

'That's good. We're good friends.'

'Yeah, right.'

'Oh, while I remember. Karen Hennessy asked after you. Give my love to Nerdo, she said.'

'Really? I could be in there with the sympathy vote.'

From Nervo's house, the Mini managed to get to Tim's road. There were kids playing everywhere and some retard had thrash metal music blaring from his open bedroom window. Tim led me around the side of his parents' house.

'Do you want coke or juice?' he asked. 'I can do milkshakes.'

'Milkshakes? Go for that, yeah.'

'What flavour?'

A girl's voice answered for me, 'Strawberry and Oreo cookie, please.'

This was Tim's sister, Andrea, stretched out on a sun lounger, her dark hair plastered to her head in a black woman's hip hop fashion with big sunglasses and little blue bikini. Tim and his sister got on well, so he set to work on his blender in the kitchen without comment. I stood there appreciating not only the sleek body of Andrea but the wonderful vision of Beth on the next lounger. She lifted her sunglasses when she realised I was there and waved.

'Do you want the same, Beth?' called Tim.

'Please.'

On close inspection, scantily clad Beth had a sheen of perspiration on her forehead, on her upper arms and on her flat belly. Andrea was fastidiously adjusting her bikini bottoms with her knees in the air. The beating I took seemed worth it to be off sick in such company.

'Alex, come and sit with me,' ordered Andrea. 'Get your top stripped off, it's a lovely day.'

I did as I was told, Tim came up with fantastic milkshakes and I sunbathed in a Hounslow garden. Tim and I were on the grass at our proper levels below the girls. I chatted away with Andrea. She was a smart girl, knowing better than to talk about her “Uni”, instead covering our shared love of Man United, music, whether she should get an Audi, her new Italian boyfriend.

‘Does he speak English?’ I asked.

I caught Tim smiling at me until Beth demanded 100% attention again.

‘Of course he speaks English.’

The music down the street which I hadn’t notice cease started up again, Andrea swinging her legs off the lounger and casting a furious look.

‘I’m going to batter that knob head,’ she said. She prodded down an edge of plaster on my arm. ‘Did you look after my baby brother?’

‘It was him who backed me up.’

‘Who are you seeing now, Alex?’

‘No-one.’

‘Not like you. Shall I fix you up?’

‘If I can’t have you, Andrea, I...’

She laughed. I don’t know what it was, but there would never be anything between me and Andrea. I could just about see her eyes watching me through the sunglasses and I thought about it again. No, still didn’t know why.

‘My friend Jennifer’s free now? No? What type do you really go for? Who is your ideal woman?’

‘Claudia Cardinale.’

‘Who the hell’s Claudia Cardinale?’

‘She’s an Italian actress from the sixties. Her or Grace Kelly. You must have heard of Grace Kelly.’

‘Oh, yeah. You’re a lost cause, Alex.’

SIX

The serious heat arrived on Sunday morning. Every other hot day that summer had simply been preparation for suffocating humidity, and so wearing just shorts I felt very uncomfortable and muggy-brained watching some raunchy woman presenting the weather on Sky news with the map of Britain inundated with yellow suns. I attempted to turn the Celsius figures into Fahrenheit but quickly gave that up as a bad job, taking a glass of cold milk out onto the stairwell. I sat without even the whiff of a cooling breeze, half my mind drawn out into the countryside and the other back at the pool table pocket. I was still to read the letter, hoping perhaps that whatever it contained was now out of date. Only briefly over the last twenty-four hours had I puzzled about it. Now I wondered why I was so reluctant to read it, having never received anything unpleasant in the post, not even a chain letter. Nobody had ever messed with me. Shot at a couple of times but that had been a random group thing on the wrong streets. A dozen fights in my life but never mugged or robbed; it had always been meaningless young violence like Friday night. I started to think of Nervo on the London pavement.

Suddenly I was on the end of a wolf whistle, and turned to see a happy Miss Brocklebank wave before jumping into her Fiat. The world's gone mad, I thought.

The Cinquecento drove off. I huffed. 'Jesus, there's no air.' I put my discomfort down to the English inability to acclimatize quickly. I would be fine in a couple of days, just as a cold front moved in.

A car could be heard coming up the side. I would have to put a tollgate down there. Nichola Duckinfield pulled in, waving and smiling while parking. For some reason I was delighted to see her, putting her shades up onto her short hair as she swung her bare legs from the car.

'Mrs Duckinfield.'

'Mr Robateau. Permission to come aboard?'

I gave an open arm gesture and she came up to sit on the top step near my bare feet. She was girlishly excited to be there, smiling up at me. She wore a flimsy khaki summer dress which allowed me to give consideration to her mildly sunburnt shoulders and collarbones, as well as the beginning curves to the top of her bosom.

'The heat's too much,' she said.

'Hottest day of the year.'

'Not working today?'

'I'm off sick.'

Straight away, I let my toes pad along her taut thigh. She watched it.

'So what's wrong with you?'

'I've been badly beaten up, with baseball bats and knives, by a gang of ten to fifteen men. I'm traumatised and looking forward to the compensation.'

'You look fine to me. I shouldn't have bothered.'

'No, no, I'm touched by your concern, really. Would you like something to drink?'

'Some juice, please.'

Returning with her drink, I found her in the other chair, so we could sit with our legs overlapping, our warm flesh gently rubbing.

'Can you remember a cold winter's day?' I asked her.

'Huh?'

'Can you remember what it was like to be so cold that it almost hurt? Imagine sitting out here dressed as we are now with it snowing. Or lying down on that piece of grass.'

'You're punch drunk, young man.'

'You can't, can you? You forget how bad last winter was just like at Christmas it will be impossible to remember this humidity. I just thought that was interesting.'

'Yes, I understand you. Which do you prefer?'

'I love snow. But this is wicked. I choose hot summer.'

'So do I. Do you get any sun around this side?'

'At about four o'clock. Do you want to stay here until then?'

'Mm, wouldn't mind.'

The physical contact was making me a little high. I had placed one of my big toes against one of her smallest and was gradually forcing it back.

'What are you doing?'

'Your toes look like they've been squashed up for years. Let me force this one back, it will feel great.'

I pressed on to just below pain.

'Oh, yes,' she said. 'That's good.'

I did the other little pinkie and then all together. She started laughing at our knees up in the air.

'Don't fight me, Nichola.'

'I'm not! It's nice, honestly.'

On Nichola's suggestion, I made myself slightly more presentable and we wandered across the road to the Red Lion, sitting in the crowded garden. It took a while for her to relax, looking around to see if anybody knew her while I watched on in amusement. Maybe she wanted somebody to see her, I thought, especially when she touched on the subject of her husband's business dilemmas and the blazing rows at their palatial spread in Richmond. Should I push for a divorce settlement? In the end she lightened up and proved to be excellent company with the conversation inevitably turning to, as she put it, "rumpy pumpy".

Back across at the flat, I declined to offer "rumpy pumpy" because it was time for cricket practice. Instead I allowed her to virtually molest me up against her car before she dragged herself away.

I dressed in sports gear and trainers and gathered up my cricket haversack. My back was much improved, if a touch uncomfortable as I drove away in my Audi, hot air coming through the vents set on cold and a nice Coldplay song on the radio. I looked at that Megane again parked near the pub, then I was out on the country roads enjoying my own vehicle. I picked up Tim and we took the short ride to the manicured grounds of the snobby Delaney School. We went through the black iron gateway and parked up on grass a good three hundred yards away from the main school buildings.

Team captain, Tony Phillips, who was a good bloke despite being an Estate Agent, was there early in his short shorts to set up the practice nets and open up the changing shack. A motley bunch of men of mixed ages gradually turned up, a few hung over and most not keen on Captain Phillips wanting to start them off with two laps of the field.

'Are you having a laugh?' asked one of the younger players. 'It's ninety degrees out here.'

Tim and I laughed at the dissent.

Phillips was on his toes, clapping his hands together, 'Come on, now.'

Being as I was in good shape I led the way, talking cricket with Phillips. Tim, who associated strenuous exercise with throwing up, trotted along at the rear.

'I wasn't born for this,' he called out at one stage.

Just as we all staggered back after the run a blue Mercedes SLK pulled up. Tony Phillips went to greet the driver and brought him over to the sweating, coughing group.

'Everyone,' said Phillips, 'this is Neil. We're giving him a try-out.'

'Hello, Neil.'

'Welcome, mate.'

'Round the fucking field.'

Everyone laughed. Neil Duckinfield put his Mercedes keys (yes, times were hard) in his pocket and moved about shaking hands. I knew who the man was when he stepped out of the car. I waited my time then gave the firmest of handshakes, noticing that I was not given any more attention than anyone else. Best not to mention squeezing his wife's toes.

Practice was played out. I took my turn to have a bat in the nets, then while Phillips organised a catching circle I went off with Tim to work on my wicket-keeping techniques. Wearing my gloves, I would take various types of throws in on the stumps and also pretend catches, Tim having me diving left and right.

'You're from Kentmere, aren't you?' said an approaching Neil Duckinfield. 'I thought I recognised you.'

I thought it best to get up from my knees.

'That's right,' I answered politely.

But that was it, Neil Duckinfield on the way to his car, 'It's a very good place,' he left me with.

'Yes, it is.'

Tim came up from his position to put a hand on my shoulder, saying, 'Jesus Christ.' I looked quickly at him, but Tim was pointing at Beth and Carla walking towards us. 'Women. It's Sunday and they still can't leave us alone.'

I watched the Mercedes drive away. I flicked sweat from my forehead and threw my gloves down on my bag. As the girls got there I playfully joined Tim in going to Beth for a hug. Unable to choose, she embraced us both together. Carla waited patiently on my sense of humour then refused my advances as I apologised. 'No, sod off. And you're not having any of the water I've brought.'

'You've got water?'

'No, you can whistle for it.'

I was pleased to see a happy Carla, giving me the fiery eyes and pout, but my attention was drawn away by the thin straps of Beth's pink thong indenting into her flesh above her jeans. I felt the urge to shake Tim by the throat until dead. I accepted the water to slake my thirst, bidding farewell as Tim slouched an arm over his girlfriend and wandered off.

'I've got better things to do,' she was moaning.

'Don't do that,' he complained as she picked at the stitches in his nose.

One of my team mates drove off with, bizarrely, Adam and the Ants booming from his convertible Peugeot. I closed up to Carla.

'Hi,' I said. 'What are we up to, then?'

'I don't know.'

'You missed practice. But don't worry, there's a match next week.'

'Deep joy.'

We just started to walk, to a different area of the picturesque school grounds. Neither of us noticed who sought out the other's hand.

'I missed you last night,' I told her.

'What, you didn't have a ready-made replacement?'

'No.'

'Well, I missed you too.'

We found some shade and lounged out together. The sound of Adam and the Ants passed over us again as the Peugeot came round the school and we both laughed.

'That should be in your car,' she told me.

I saw that we had come down into a hollow, obscured from the cricket field and the school buildings, and a thick hedge between the oak trees hid us from the road. She was sitting up, picking at blades of grass, her wild hair flopping at the side of her face. She wore a sleeveless white top, allowing me to admire her toned and tanned shoulders.

'Did you come in Beth's car?'

'Yeah.'

'So I'm stuck with you now?'

'Looks like it.'

'Well, you're cooking tea.'

She blew hair out of her eyes and dispensed with the grass on her fingers. She seemed to like it there as well, quiet except for a passing motorbike. I crawled towards her and used my superior weight to gently press her down into the bank. There was a little gasp from her, but no objection and then a smile. My face filled her world as I considered whether or not I should kiss her and just exactly where I should kiss her. It was mutually pleasant anyway, all the right chemicals flying around. I knew it was perfect out there, a clear sky, dry comfortable grass. She was cute, all submissive below me, smelling so nice, yet I still found myself thinking of her as a friend. What the hell, I just had to taste her, closing my mouth on hers with full passion, feeling all her body respond and her hands move up my back. I paused briefly, asking, 'Are we cool with this?'

'Of course.'

The kissing became intense, on to cheeks and necks, and back to gasping mouths. She became aware that my erection was trapped in the wrong direction, so in an unselfish act she went into my trackie bottoms to rectify the situation, and felt unable to then release me. I was undoing her fly-button jeans with one hand.

'Can I touch you?' I whispered to her ear.

'Yes.'

I slipped my hand inside her panties, trying suddenly not to think of Beth's thong, desperately trying not to think of that, then I was pleasing this girl who was my lovely friend as she continued to move her hand on me with surprising gentleness.

'Let's do it,' she gasped.

I disowned her as a friend as she started to push my trousers down my body. The kissing continued. As I moved the material of her underwear aside Adam Ant came back demanding that we stand and deliver, making us both dissolve into hysterics.

'The fucker's lost,' I said, still giggling.

'Who is he?'

'I don't know. He's a friend of the captain.'

We stayed in that position for a moment, both amused, her waiting and me feeling an attack of conscience.

'Oh, Jesus Christ, Carla. What are we going to do?'

'Errm, carry on would be a good idea.'

'I can't do that.'

Slowly she covered us both up and simply held me.

'Sorry,' I finally said against her shoulder.

She kissed my cheek, quite content. I showed my face and apologised again.

'It's all right, Alex. This is normal for me.'

'Normal? Carla, I don't know what's going on with me. You're gorgeous, and I do want to do what we just didn't do.'

'Hey, it's just the friends thing. What if I do something nasty to you and then we can just get on with it.'

'You couldn't do anything nasty.'

'Oh, yeah? What if I scratch a key down the side of your car? Or..?'

I was kissing her again.

'I don't want to think about this,' I said. 'Shall we just go with the flow? Friends that don't have to ask. Everything's fine. Everything goes, well, not in the swinging sense, but do you know what I'm saying? If it happens, it happens, and we don't have to keep wondering how the other person's feeling.'

She was giving me a "you're scaring me" expression. I stopped myself and got up, dragging her with me.

'Make yourself decent, woman.'

'I looked fine 'til you jumped me.'

'Come on.'

I led her up to the cricket fields which were now occupied by dog walkers. We went hand in hand to my car.

SEVEN

I was not surprised that Karen Hennessy had become disillusioned with where her office was situated in central London, as the view from her window consisted almost entirely of a Sainsbury's car park.

'Look at those idiots,' she said, meaning the noon-day shoppers moving in a heat haze across the tarmac.

I desisted from staring at Karen's trendy meant-to-be-seen bra through her flimsy white blouse and glanced outside.

'I saw it in the park yesterday with Cameron,' she continued. 'All the bare flesh burning away. Next time I go into the Club changing rooms half the women will be as red as beetroots.

Being as brown as an African myself I declined to comment, looking again instead through the glass partition to where Karen's three female agents beavered away on the phones with a bank of photos of the young models behind them. One of the agents turned; she was pretty and had her hair parted in the middle and pulled down in bunches just like the girl from Mrs B's, just like Joely's.

'Bless them,' said Karen. 'The money-making models, not my staff.'

Karen tidied her desk before we left.

'You were a model, of course, weren't you, Karen?'

'Yes, for a few years, until husband No.1. came along. Protection of the skin was drummed into me as a model.'

'I take it you don't go to Spain for your holidays.'

'Oh, I do, for Cameron. But I take care. Husband No.2. was a skiing fanatic, so all the sun at the top of mountains, as well.'

One of the girls knocked and looked in, sniffling a cold into a tissue, apologetic for disturbing the boss. She had the gorgeous round face of a model that I could easily imagine securing lipstick adverts, etc, but a body like a bag of spanners kept her in the office.

'It's all right, Sue,' said Karen.

'It's Mr Madders on the phone,' Sue said through her bunged up nose. 'He's being very insistent.'

'Will you excuse me for a second, Alex?'

I nodded and watched Karen follow Sue out and across the office to the phone. She had a brief, very animated conversation, with a quick glance in my direction and a pull on an ear-ring, then she returned and popped her head in to me.

'Let's go to lunch,' she said with a smile.

A couple of insane joggers from the gym delayed my entry to Kentmere after a nice lunch with Karen. With it being stiflingly hot again, I considered them to be complete and utter nut jobs. I thought the same of the tennis players I could see, and also of myself for having to work in such heat. I made it into the shade as quickly as possible, letting on to some familiar staff. Tim stood waiting for me when I got to the office. He was in khaki shorts, white tee-shirt and red neckerchief, as if he were in some old Humphrey Bogart movie.

'Beth bit me,' he said, not even bothering to pretend it was for wiping away the sweat of a day's toil.

'Has Tuohy seen you like that?'

'I don't give a fuck. I'm not wearing dungarees in this heat. No, I did see him and he was fine about it. Seems to have stopped being an arsehole for some reason.'

General Manager Tommy Macro filled the doorway.

'Who's stopped being an arsehole?' he asked in a friendly way.

'Nervo,' answered Tim. 'His battering sorted him out.'

'Right. Good. Alex, I've had a complaint that the disabled bays are wearing away. Do you think you could sort it out?'

'Of course, yeah. I'll do it as soon as I can today.'

'Thank you.' He noticed the plaster on my arm. 'Is that okay?'

'That? Yes. I should take it off now, really.'

Macro nodded at us and moved off down the corridor. Tim indicated his nose and mimed a "what about me, you fucker?"

Naturally, we brewed up before we did anything. The first job had us helping the leisure staff take in delivery of a new rowing machine. Another cup of tea was needed after that sweaty palaver, then we split up, Tim salvaging Nervo's flowerbeds that had been damaged by some Saturday night horseplay, and I out into the sun to assess the disabled parking paint job. I was unimpressed with the standard of the work to begin with, but decided that I should be able to rectify it.

In a squeal of rubber, a bartender arrived on his bicycle, bringing Carla to mind. I had to smile, thinking about Carla because she was also a bartender and not as the local “bike”. I looked around for her car and found it. The previous day had been nice, hanging out with her at the flat, the sexual tension almost done with. She had cooked me crappy economy burgers from the shop and we then sat outside drinking wine as the evening finally cooled and a huge red sun slowly sank away. Later, we decamped to the sofa to listen to music and talk. With more wine and cheeky banter she had eventually moved into my arms, both now accepting that it was best not to go any further. In fact I was beginning to prefer the emotional fun of a cuddle to sex. We remained there warm together, talking quietly, until bedtime came around. She had used the bathroom first while I stood on the stairs enjoying the relief of the cool night, listening to Spandau Ballet drifting along from Miss Brocklebank’s.

‘All yours,’ called Carla.

I turned to watch her pad over to me wearing just a yellow tee-shirt. She gave me a noisy kiss and we bid each other goodnight.

What a tumultuous couple of days, I thought. I was happy to have Carla there and it was turning into a summer to remember. I thought back to my best summers. They seemed to come in seven year jumps. There was the time spent with Rob Cross as fourteen-year-olds diving into Salford Quays during the day and then diving into Sharon Grundy from Stretford during the evenings. Then at twenty-one, a two week holiday on Ibiza turned into a month as I got with a girl who it turned out knew Sharon Grundy from Stretford. I was feeling fourteen once more as Carla returned for a glass of water and I gave her another goodnight peck on the cheek.

The flashing and click of the central locking of a red Ferrari brought me out of my reverie. Tommy Macro was there smiling at me. 'Is it going to be a problem after all?'

'What, boss?'

'The disabled markings.'

'Oh, that, no trouble. I was just miles away. New car?'

'No, I've had it a while. Normally I'm in the Jag.' We both stood appreciating it. 'Any time you want to borrow it, just... don't ask.'

I watched Macro drive out and roar off down the road. I could still hear the engine fifteen seconds later. Then Brendan Tuohy was there, with his pale complexion and limp grey suit. I wanted to punch him even before he spoke.

'Are we making progress here?'

'Just about to, Mr Tuohy.'

'Very good. Carry on.'

He minced away across the car-park, getting into his bog-standard white Peugeot 405 without even taking his jacket off. I headed back in, watching Tuohy leave over my shoulder. 'Who's running the fucking ship?'

Late in the afternoon the staff room began to take on the appearance of a casualty department after a major incident. There were bartenders and gym assistants sprawled out on the floor, some pressing their bare backs against the metal lockers which were supposed to be cool. Most were drinking water or coke, not many talking except for a receptionist on the phone. Tim and I were in the corner, drained and just waiting to stop sweating before we went home.

A flushed Carla came in with Libby from Admin and they both sat down on the cigarette-marked carpet. Right behind them came the sour-faced Rachel Calderbank, stepping over legs to get to her locker as if they were patches of dog mess, then leaving without a word.

'Timmy, get us some water,' ordered Libby.

'Yeah, like that's going to happen,' he replied deadpan.

Carla reached forward to grab my leg. 'Alex, come down in the sauna with me.'

I looked at her aghast. 'Are you off your fucking head?'

'Come on, you can't get any hotter. Then we can go in the plunge pool.'

'We're not allowed in the Wet room at this time.'

'We are when there's no members in. The whole place is empty.'

I was quickly coerced. Tim was invited too.

'Only if Libby goes in the nuddie.'

'Yeah, that's going to happen,' she threw back at him.

I left Tim where he lay and met up with Carla again a few minutes later in the Wet room. I always had trunks in my locker and she was in a black bikini. At first I thought the sauna was going to kill me but soon adapted and relaxed. Carla was stretched out on the level below me, a film of wetness across her body.

'Hey, Carla.'

'Mm?'

'Married couples spend less time together than us.'

'That's true.'

I shifted position, letting my eyes move over her with admiration but no longer with lustful intent. She was just Carla again now and I hoped to sustain the relationship for a long time. Oddly, Will Young's song *Evergreen* started to be pumped into the sauna, possibly someone on the Leisure desk hitting the wrong switch. It stirred Carla, turning to be propped up on one elbow.

'Are you taking me out tonight?' she asked.

'Ah, I wish I could, but I don't want to.'

'It's another woman, isn't it?'

'You've put me off women for life. No, I'm planning on putting a mattress on my stairs, drinking obscene amounts of alcohol and staying there until it cools down.'

We remained in the sauna another ten minutes, listening to Will and then Celine Dion. Geri Halliwell was going a bit too far. 'Oh, Jesus Christ,' I said.

I led the way to the plunge pool and we both joyfully went down in that. We simultaneously pushed a hand over our soaking heads and laughed, Carla making a big O with her mouth at the sensation of the water. We both bobbed towards each other, softly docking against the side wall. I was already serious and her smile turned into resigned acceptance that this was as intimate as we would ever be.

'Can I book you for next summer?' she asked.

'You can, madam. I'll be doing tours next year.'

On the way out, I bumped into Tim again and we shared a couple of covert cans of Stella just inside the staff entrance. Still legal but feeling light-headed I drove home, hauling myself up the stairs in need of instant food. It was a choice of Pot Noodle or an omelette, so went for the second option, cooking it as Delia Smith says.

I sat with my food and iced water just inside the open doorway, hiding away from the still hot sun low in the west, and not wanting to overlook Miss Brocklebank washing her Fiat in saggy pale green tracksuit. At last a breeze moved around the flat, bringing with it a train horn far in the distance. Suddenly, I put my plate down and stood up to the pool table, pulling that bastard letter out from within the money.

Alex,

This money is yours for reading this letter. It is anonymous, of course, the reason becoming clear later. My investigations have confirmed what I already suspected, that you are the right man for a job I require doing. Before I give you the proposition I think it important to tell you the fee: £100,000. The cash will be delivered the same way as the first as your Landlord seems an upstanding man, and will come before, yes before, the job once you have chosen to accept it. The job, for £100,000, is murder. Whether or not you have screwed up this letter you will keep reading.

As adrenalin coursed through me my fingers tensed enough to scrunch up the paper but it remained open for me to read on.

A stranger on stranger murder is clearly the safest way to avoid detection, as long as you take measure not to leave any obvious evidence or get caught in the act. In the same respect the best way to avoid prosecution for conspiracy to commit murder is not to be known to the murderer. So that takes a lot of trust. I will not risk a murder charge by paying the local thug, who botches the job and then spills his guts. But I will risk a conspiracy to commit grievous bodily harm charge if you double-cross me.

You have 28 days to make your decision from receiving this letter. You should show a sign of acceptance. I think it would be dramatic to swap the flag at your place of work. I will look every day and send the fee as soon as I see a different flag. If for some reason this is not practical, then put a flag in your window above the road. The second envelope will contain the fee and all the information you require to do the job. If no sign is shown then you will never hear from me again.

After accepting the job you will have 28 days to complete it before the local thug moves in for five grand. If you vanish, then he will go for friends and family. I have addresses in Hounslow, Gorton and Salford. Is this some sort of set-up, you may ask. Well you know the police are not allowed to do this. Why would anyone else? You will quickly discount this. Would I grass you up? An unsolved murder (the majority, despite what Crimewatch says) will quickly go away, especially if it appears to be a botched robbery. If you are arrested, then the police come after anyone with a connection to the victim.

Again common sense.

So to recap. £100,000 cash upfront to kill a complete stranger. No connection with me protects both of us. 28 days to show a sign of acceptance. 28 days to do the job after receiving fee and details. That simple.

Thank you for your time.

Now my heart was going like a jackhammer inside my chest. Sweat welled on my eyebrows and streamed from my armpits. My first thought was if this was my reaction to just reading an offer, how could I ever carry through on such an act. Move around, I told myself, get the blood doing something. I started to pace the flat, dropping the letter when I realised I still had hold of it. I felt like swearing but that was coming up from somewhere else, somewhere outside. It was both male and female voices at the rear of the building, proving too strong even at that crazy moment for me to ignore. I gradually peered over the parapet to see a small white van. The argument was between Miss Brocklebank and a bullish shaven-headed man who threw the stepladders he was holding to the floor with a clatter as he swore at her again. Had she forgotten to pay the window cleaner?

'Are you all right, Miss Brocklebank?' I called down.

'Oh, yes. It's my boyfriend. Everything's fine.'

'Yeah, so take it back inside, mate,' said the man.

I waited for a nod from Miss Brocklebank before taking it back inside, relieved not to have to tangle with the man. I listened for a few minutes as the row cooled to a heated debate and then to quiet. Now I was left in silence again, knowing that nothing I could do would postpone the intense consultation to be had on "who and why". I just had to decide where this would take place. I could go out on my bike or in the car. Maybe I could walk up to the church or down to the canal.

I started to feel the onset of a siege mentality, not wanting to go out at all now, so locked the door and eventually went through to the bathroom. I stripped and put the shower on with lukewarm water, having a token wash before sitting down with the jet gently flowing off my head. I had a vision of Miss Brocklebank being strangled at that very moment and then admonished myself for thinking of murder.

I was not sure how long I spent in the shower. No answers had been forthcoming, no conclusion on how I felt about somebody coming at me with such a proposal. Wearing just trackie bottoms I knelt on the mat and sent the ball against the wall without my gloves. I took most returns subconsciously, focussing once as it was heading for my eyes. I upped the pace, the der-do sound taking on an aggressive rhythm as I took balls high and low, my hands starting to throb. Then a ball hit a piece of chipped brickwork and shot through right onto my groin. I was pole-axed for a second as the pain raced down my legs and into my stomach, then I started to laugh uncontrollably as I lay curled up on the mat, my eyes and nose running and my face feeling dusty.

Now here was something you don't see every day; at the sound of a car horn I looked in the mirror to see the driver of a BMW, furious at my letting in two cars at a junction, swearing at me and giving me very expressive dual wanker hand gestures, looking remarkably like he was beating a drum for the Roman Empire. I felt my blood pressure shoot up and, whereas only two days before I would have been out of the car, I just drove on, gradually calming and not wanting to show the man the error of his ways.

I had gone without sleep, pacing my flat in a blur of worry and paranoia, focussing on no particular aspect of the situation and finishing by watching the sun rise over the Red Lion while drinking strong coffee. It was another Tuesday, and I intended to behave completely normally, by visiting my solid friend Nervo and having a laugh at work with Tim and any other member of staff. I would go up to Carla and hug her and thank her for being who she was. Maybe that wasn't being normal, but it was a glorious day and I was going to enjoy it. There would be no annoyance with oddball tennis players or stupid management. And definitely no flirtation with wealthy women. Just a regular, no stress, no complications Tuesday.

Relatively content and clear in my mind as to my immediate plan of action, I'd cleaned up, feeling lousy of course, found my sunglasses as a matter of urgency, and drove out. My glances left and right were far more comprehensive than usual. That silver Renault Megane was there again near the pub. I would be asking the Landlady, Mrs Lennox, about it. But not today. Not on this Tuesday.

On arrival at Nervo's in Hounslow, I came across a

gang of teenagers kicking several footballs across the No Ball Games green in front of his house. One of the balls dropped in my territory.

'Ee, ar, mate,' called one of the players. 'Give it your best shot.'

I had not played football for about five years. I swung my right foot but the heavy casey only did a short Barnes Wallis to the middle of the grass. I ignored the blunt appraisal of my talent and found my friend gardening down the side of the house. Nervo was pleasantly surprised to see me. We had breakfast together on his Ground Force decking and I enjoyed hearing moans and worries from the man, although much of it passed me by in my trance-like state.

'Well?' he asked.

'Well what?'

'I was talking about wanting to get back to work.'

That set me thinking about taking some important time away from things.

'Are you sure? You shouldn't rush back.'

'I knew you'd try to stop me, but honestly, Alex, I feel fine. I'll come back tomorrow.'

'Well,' I took the last croissant, 'if you insist.'

EIGHT

On arrival home from work on that Tuesday night, I left my trainers and socks to their own devices outside the door and scurried away from the still burning sun. In the company of a can of strong lager I took a long cooling shower. Then, as I prepared my evening meal, I listened to the three messages on the phone. The first was Karen Hennessy suggesting a picnic.

'Picnic?' I said to myself.

I had not been on a picnic since... ever. Adolescent drinking in the park was the closest I'd come to it. Still, I decided it might have been pleasant, last week, but not now. The second message was, bizarrely, Nichola Duckinfield suggesting a picnic. Maybe it was picnic week in the Rich people's social calendar. The last message was Carla, playfully annoyed that a long text to me was now void as she had realised I was still to get a new mobile. I rang her back, asking where she was.

'I'm round at my dad's. Why, do you want to do something?'

'Not at the moment. How about a picnic tomorrow?'

'*What*?'

'Nothing. Where were you today?'

'I was there. You didn't look very hard, did you?'

'Write me a letter.'

'*What*?'

'With whatever was in the text.'

'Don't be stupid. Get off your arse and get a mobile.'

'Oh, that's charming, that is. Here's me, slaving away all day.'

'Slaving, my arse.'

I kidded with her. 'If you say arse again I'm going to hang up.'

'Alex, what's this picnic business? Do you want to sit outside for lunch tomorrow?'

'I'm not in tomorrow.'

'There you go, I rest my case, you arse.'

'Right, that's it, I'm going.'

'No, sorry,' she laughed. 'Let's keep talking.'

'My food's ready. I'll catch you Thursday.'

'Thursday? Okay, see you Thursday.'

'Goodnight, Carla.'

'Goodnight, Arse.'

I spent the evening lounged on the sofa, drinking beer, watching a couple of films and then went to bed late. I found it was now my habit to scan the street before retiring, and my village stood deserted apart from a fox on a mission.

I was riding my bicycle home from school when the banging started. I could see the faces of old school buddies and recognised the green bubble-jacket I was wearing, and my breath visible over my cold hands on the Grifter's handlebars. The banging brought me round, allowing the dream to be filed away, alongside my current favourite of making love to ex-girlfriend Chloe. The present-day was a disappointment after the joy of childhood, with the noise only being a knocking at the door. Suddenly I was tense, bouncing out of bed to look out again with squinting eyes onto another hot Surrey morning, but seeing nothing unusual. A peek out from the bedroom showed a glimpse of Karen Hennessy through the square window in the back door. Should I have pretended not to be home? That might have an over-excited Mike Yu offering to let her in fearing a tragedy, and besides, I wanted to see her. I would keep my head down for a while but would not start playing silly buggers entirely with my normal life. I threw on some clothes before answering the door.

'What a lovely day for a picnic,' I said.

'I wasn't sure if it was your scene, Alex.'

'Oh, sure, I love to picnic. There will be cheap cider involved?'

She took me to a magnificent Stately Home, which I didn't ask the name of, with its rolling lawns, roaming deer and all. I felt slightly silly lugging the hamper across the grass but after we were settled down I relaxed and quickly ignored the wandering day-trippers and rabbit droppings. Karen had made the effort with the food, or at least her cook had, with the Mexican chicken looking particularly appealing and an obviously expensive wine which I also didn't care to identify.

I lounged there enjoying the perfect temperature and with the soothing smell of burning wood in the air. I watched Karen playing mother, her sleek legs tucked underneath her and her shoulders taut over the hamper. I found myself really looking at her for the first time. On face value she was striking, but then I disregarded the haughty arrogance of wealth and her flirtatious attentions that had teased my ego, and could tell that ultimately she was not to be trusted. It was in the eyes, almost imperceptible, but it was there. A coldness that no amount of money or grooming could disguise. She suddenly reminded me of my Aunt Cath from Gorton (financial status aside) who lived a contented life of Bingo and the Local, always with a houseful of kids and neighbours, who wouldn't hesitate to use the words Meningitis and Pendlebury Children's Hospital the moment she wanted time to pay a bill or a favour from a tradesman. It was the kind of deviousness I sensed in Karen Hennessy.

I accepted more wine and berated myself for thinking too much. What could Karen Hennessy do to me? She moved closer, talking about the early days of seeing me around the club. I smiled when she mentioned a buxom woman I knew who had been press-ganged into a game of tennis. Karen started to use her eyes on me and I had to admit I could see no demons there. Maybe I was just getting carried away with the letter business. I mentioned Nervo.

'Oh!' she said, acknowledging her mistake with his name.

I recounted the time Nervo had commented on Karen. 'Nervo said, "I could have had a woman like that, if I had something about me".'

We both laughed. She was closer, clamping down on her bottom lip, a slight sheen either side of her slim nose. I felt an involuntary stirring of the loins. Surely she would not initiate anything out there, despite the surroundings being lovely. I even got a warm smile from a passing granny.

'Do you like France?' Karen asked.

'Do I like France? Yes, I like France.'

'Have you ever been?'

'I have, actually. To watch United. Didn't take in much culture, though.'

'I've got some property in the Pyrenees. A converted barn. Perhaps we could go sometime?'

'Perhaps we could.'

She extracted a kiss.

'Are you due any holidays from the club?'

'We don't really do holidays. We just don't show up.'

We were sharing slow kisses.

'Alex, I meant to ask you. Why do you work there? I mean, you could be so much more.'

'Like what, a lawyer? A doctor? I'm lazy, Karen.'

'You're not lazy. I've seen the way you work. Actually, I've stared at the way you work.'

'Anyway, I've taken too many wrong turns since school. I'm not chasing anything more than I've already got.'

Her hands were on my inner thigh and she was caressing her cheek down with the grain of my facial stubble.

'Are you going to jump me right here?' I asked.

'Of course not,' she teased. 'Do you think I'm some kind of exhibitionist?'

Within the hour we were at Karen's home in Walton-on-Thames. She ignored her elderly neighbours with their menagerie of at least five dogs and a donkey, so I ignored them also. Karen disappeared for a while upstairs, leaving me to take the solo tour, liking the Egyptian artefacts in the spacious lounge, and then the novelty of the glass covered well in the middle of the oak floor, but especially the wall of arty-farty photos of naked models.

'The one in the centre is my daughter,' said Karen coming in with drinks.

'*What*?' I asked, a little stunned, craning forward for a closer look before correcting myself.

Basically it was a bum shot, a very toned woman of about twenty with her back to the camera, long sleek legs akimbo a glass case.

'Is that a python?'

'Mmm, I think so. More wine?'

'Thanks.'

'She's the result of my first marriage. There were no other positives. Shall we go outside?'

I dragged myself away from Karen's naked daughter and accepted a sun lounger on a trellised patio. The garden stretched on forever and was a jungle all the way. She tutted when I mentioned that "Nerdo" would be horrified by it.

'That poor man,' she said. 'What must he think of me?'

'Give over, you couldn't care less about Nervo.'

'True.'

She placed a cushion on the ground and dropped to a kneeling position between my feet, propped up on my thighs with her chin held on very floppy feminine wrists. I played with her hair.

'Did you enjoy the picnic?'

'Yes. Thank you for asking me.'

'My pleasure.'

The sounds of Eminem suddenly destroyed the ambience of the country garden.

'Delinquents at The Beeches,' she explained after another tut. I remembered the anti-social summer music from Tim's neighbour and imagined Andrea saying "delinquents at the Beeches".

Karen stroked my tanned forearms. 'You should take more care in the sun.'

'Thank you for your concern.'

'I'm serious. It can be very damaging.'

Eminem was cut off in mid-rant, replaced by a dirty Christina Aguilera. Karen very deliberately began a slow undoing of the studs of my jeans, allowing enough time for my arousal as I watched her delicate fingers and subconsciously waddled for a more comfortable position. Karen almost gasped as I sprang free into her hands. An Alicia Keys track took over the airways. Karen said, 'I hope they find something I can work to.' I started to smile as Karen devoured me whole, rolling her eyes upwards after a few moments to stare at me, clearly determined to do a thoroughly professional job. I moved left and right for the best view, then had to look away as Karen went at it hammer and tongs. I inadvertently laughed out loud. With a start I became aware of being watched from over the left garden fence. It was a sideways glance from a big glassy brown eye, watching on with cold indifference. I decided against enquiring whether Karen knew the name of next door's donkey, and simply winked at the animal. I smiled and looked away, straight into the face of Karen's French Au Pair, standing in the doorway to the kitchen. She had clearly not just arrived home, wearing a pinny with flour on her face and hair. She was not shocked by what was going on, her face as impassive as the donkey's. Had she been there long? Had Karen really not known she was in? Were we having rock cakes for tea?

It was still hot on Thursday, so hot as to dull concentration, but even so driving my Audi I could not stop that bastard letter rushing around my mind again. I made Aerosmith bang out of the rear speakers and took the car up to fifty, but it was getting me going once more. As it transpired, spending most of the previous day with Karen Hennessy had proved to be the perfect distraction. So, if Nichola Duckinfield had been spotted around the grounds, I might have taken her up on her picnic offer. I wondered if that would include providing a floor show for the hired help. Maybe I should just give all my attention to Carla; after all she would be gone again soon. Thinking of Carla calmed me down.

I pulled into Kentmere and parked as close to the lime green Beetle as possible. The white gravel acted as a sun trap and I squinted at Carla skipping towards me in a happy mood.

'Hiya, you,' she said, giving me a lovely little hug.

'All right, darling.'

Her smile slipped as she sensed my pensive frame of

mind.

'What's new?'

'I'm thinking of doing one. Do you want to take me back to "Uni" with you?'

'Are you serious?'

I rubbed my head and looked around the place. 'I don't know.' Up on the balcony I noticed Tommy Macro motionless against the railing watching us. 'We should go in.'

'Okay, but find me for a break. I'll cheer you up.'

'Young lady!' called an approaching Brendan Tuohy. 'Your shift started ten minutes ago.'

'My fault,' I interceded, hands up in surrender.

'She's been talking to other people long before you arrived.'

I watched Carla's happy mood evaporate and then tried to decide where to put my elbow on Tuohy's face.

'*She's* got a name,' I barked at the man.

Tuohy flustered and backed away with a glance at his watch. Then he turned on his heels and minced away to the main building. I glared after him, then shot a look up to Macro, then felt my hand taken into Carla's. She was smiling up at me, playfully mocking my chivalry. I snapped out of it and laughed with her.

'Well,' I said as we came in off the car-park. 'The snotty little man got my dander up.'

We ran the gauntlet of nosey staff in the doorway, hearing a couple of "you should have knocked him out, Alex" on the way through, coming to a stop on a deserted corridor in a pocket of cool air. I pressed my back against the bare wall, suddenly strained and distressed, rubbing my eyes before focussing on the lovely girl with me. Her body language, with hands in back pockets and an expression as coy as Princess Diana, suggested she just wanted to stay with me and not go to work. I gently pulled her in by the waist and she was happy to be held. She mumbled something into my shoulder.

'What?'

'I thanked you for sticking up for me.'

'You're welcome.'

She mumbled something else.

'Now what was that?'

'I said you should have knocked him out.'

That tickled me and I roared with laughter while she giggled, and it was just what I needed. I kissed her forehead and held her closer.

'Hey,' came from a passing Harry Madox, 'That's... very, very cheeky.'

'Was that Harry?' asked Carla.

'Yeah. Listen, so what are we gonna do? If I stay here it means you've got to stay here too.'

'I beg your pardon? I thought you were coming back with me.'

'What would I do there? It'll be full of "Uni" twats called Nigel.'

'Alex Robateau, you say some weird shit at times.'

'I, er... I have to agree with you, Miss Jones.' I found my best Leonard Rossiter impersonation, 'Miss Jones.'

Carla's forehead crinkled. 'What *are* you talking about?'

'Rising Damp. You've never heard of Rising Damp?'

'No.'

We laughed a little more before she had to make a move.

'I'd better join Harry.'

'Okay.'

'We'll carry on with this later.'

I let her slip from my fingers and watched her walk along the corridor until the door closed.

I headed to the office, to be met by raised voices.

'What's wrong?' I asked Tim, with Nervo in the shower.

'It's that Nimrod stressing about the Fun Day.'

'I was just saying,' Nervo called, 'I've got a wedding on the afternoon of the Fun Day, so we'll have to set up early.'

'Here you go,' said Tim, offering me a cup of tea. 'Saw you pull in. I thought you were about to knock Too High out.'

'I'm off to do him in a minute.'

I kept trying to concentrate on the matter at hand, I really did, but found myself thinking about anything but. Even so, I was permanently on edge, fretting, suffering a kind of moral nausea. The spectre of that letter was with me, but I was thinking in a whirl about women and about Nervo going to that wedding and about Carla's legs and about Manchester City's latest prima donna signing. Maybe the problem of the deal on offer was too ludicrous to consider. Or maybe I didn't have a problem. A problem would be if I wasn't living the life of Riley in the country and failing to get my head round the madness in the first place. Sky Movies and my fish supper broke up my deliberations still further on a Saturday evening spent alone for a change.

My door was open to a warm summer night, and I put up with the occasional train and Miss Brocklebank starting on a Phil Collins phase. The wedding Nervo was to attend on the club Fun Day kept nagging away at me, and then I remembered there were nuptials in my own family some time that month. I dug out the invitation and it was for the following Wednesday and I did not want to go. But then I thought about my family, and I definitely did not want to go. Apart from my father and my sister Michelle, as well as some of the Oldies, they were all scumbags. The Groom was my cousin Warren, the kind of guy who could get arrested for ABH on the way to the reception.

I knew I would have to go to the wedding; my sister would expect it and, sure enough, on the Sunday she rang to remind me. Michelle was in good health, still working as a hairdresser and dating a rugby league player. I was told I was probably billeted at my Nan's house and what time to be up in Manchester. She asked if I was bringing anyone. I thought of Carla and said I might be. I rang Carla straight away on her mobile and the first thing she said was, 'What kind of idiots get married on a Wednesday?'

'You wouldn't believe.'

'Well, Alex, I'd love to come. Thanks. Where is it?'

'The wedding is in a place called Hyde. It's where that Doctor Shipman worked.'

'Oh, charming.'

'I don't know where the reception is. Probably in some Scout hut.'

'Are we staying in a hotel?'

'No, no, but I'll make sure you're comfortable.'

'I'm excited already.'

NINE

Carla came to stay with me on the Tuesday night before the wedding. Her smile, as she stepped from her Beetle, added the final touch to what had become the perfect early evening, comfortable as I was outside with a beer, the temperature just right with the sun hazed behind thin cloud and, best of all, Barbra Streisand playing softly from next door.

'Do you want a hand?' I called down, getting even more comfy.

She waved at being all right, then trotted up with luggage and her outfit in its travel cover and gave me a peck on the cheek.

'I'm still excited,' she said.

I laughed. 'That'll soon turn into, "I'm still disgusted".'

She made herself at home. After dinner we cheerfully played ball, shot some pool, watched a film. Later on, while I returned to my lounger to continue beer drinking, Carla carried out lengthy ablutions – bathing, washing her hair etc. I fought the urge to wash her back for her, and she finally appeared in just a dressing-gown, but only to say good-night. We kissed on the lips and I said I would wake her in good time for the big day.

I was pleased that in the morning it was overcast, knowing there was nothing worse than being all suited up on a scorching hot day (Manchester Crown Court, June

2001). As I loaded the boot of my Audi, Carla came bounding down the stairs making a squeaky throaty noise of longing at me in my shorts and Chicago Bears vest. She was travelling up to Manchester in tracksuit and baseball cap, looking like a film star about to go into make-up. I got the door for her, ran around to the drivers side and we were off to the motorway.

I headed northwards as quickly as possible with the windows down a fraction to give us noisy refreshing gusts of air. After driving at very high speed, interspersed with a few stops, we finally came off the motorway at the Manchester Airport Hilton, Carla marvelling at an overloaded PIA Jumbo Jet only just managing to get airborne while I checked out the house of some relatives on the Woodhouse Park estate. We soon hit Princess Parkway and I reminisced to Carla about heady days watching United dominate City at the old Maine Road stadium. She was more interested to be riding through gangland Moss Side, and then we were in the City Centre and not long after pulling into my sister Michelle's road in Cheetham Hill. Coming from Surrey, I immediately noticed the excessive amounts of litter, as well as the traffic calming measures being well over the top. The old, terraced street was packed out with cars. Even though it was still early, Reggae music filled the air. I recognised various male cousins malingering near my sister's house, one of them practising his hard man spitting routine, and then there were loud welcoming shouts and the handshakes as I approached with Carla. My sister Michelle was to be seen through the open front door giving out instructions to young family members. Hopefully they were to decorate the hall because it was a right tip. Being a hairdresser, Michelle's dark locks were immaculately cut and the main feature everyone associated with Michelle was her perfect smile which she flashed on seeing me. I was embraced and then Carla was hugged without formality and helped in with her stuff.

'Come here,' said Michelle, grabbing me again. 'How are you doing?'

'Great, Sis. Have you got the Megane yet?'

'Oh, yeah, I wish.'

Her boyfriend, I assumed from his athletic build, came into the hall to take part in the get-together. He was introduced as Dale from the Wolves, although I had no idea whether the Wolves were Wakefield, Wigan or Warrington, and I was surprised that for a rugby league player he had gorgeous curly blond hair that needed a David Beckham hair band. I took an instant apathetic disposition towards him, with his broad Lancashire accent and his probable habit of pissing in the wardrobe after a lad's night out.

The morning took on a frenzied mode of dressing and grooming, where Carla met only a handful of my more reserved relatives, and then there was a convoy of taxis up into the hills to Hyde, to a nice old church that the bride's side had chosen.

I walked hand in hand with Carla, behind Michelle and Dale from the Wolves. Michelle's skirt was a little too short and Dale from the Wolves walked as if he had two rugby balls for testicles. In the churchyard more relatives acknowledged me as a wanderer returned and smiled warmly at my “girlfriend”. Carla, in pastel pink dress and sandals, and glowing with youthful beauty, played the role well. She whispered how much she loved weddings, what a nice setting it was and thanked me for bringing her.

Not being a big fan of weddings, I was glad to get back out of the church, even into the ritual madness of everyone gathering to see the Bride and Groom emerge. Cousin Warren was now married to Lynne from Stalybridge and I watched his shaven head and his cheeky grin as the photographer took them off to a quiet part of the grounds.

The Reception had taken over a nearby pub. Carla and I were among the first to start on the Bucks Fizz. I found a beam to lean on and Carla leant on me as we watched the rabble that is my family stream noisily in.

‘Right, stay away from her,’ I joked.

‘Stop it,’ Carla said with a stamp on my toes.

‘No, seriously, she’ll have fleas. You know those “How Clean Is Your House” programmes, they should do hers. Oh, here’s Auntie Judy and her boyfriend, Fat Boy Fat we call him.’ Carla was giggling. ‘Stepping in now are Hilda and Brian, the oldest Swingers in town.’

A handsome trio of brothers came in, cheerfully talking, but oozing menace nevertheless. Carla asked me who they were but I didn’t answer, just returned their friendly nods and winks in my direction. A gaggle of sexy girls came in who I didn’t know, and then some of the oldies had made it across.

When my Nan arrived with a lady companion I led

Carla over to meet her. My Nan was a healthy and feisty old girl who was delighted to see me and gave me a big hug. She checked me over and introduced me to her friend, then she kissed Carla and insisted we stayed at hers that night. Suddenly I was a little excluded as the two old ladies chatted with the excited Carla about the wedding and where she was from.

Michelle and Dale from the Wolves came in with my old Dad. He was a handsome grey-haired old bugger, though no longer in the best of health and leaning on Michelle's arm. My father had come across for the reception from the bungalow he shared platonically with a lady friend in Stockport. I admonished myself for being down in leafy Surrey and determined to come up for a visit after getting Carla home, other matters permitting, I added. My father's dominating shoulders from heavy work and amateur boxing now seemed a terrible burden to him and as I approached I was distressed to see that his face was rather gaunt. We embraced and of course the first thing he asked about was his son's health. I got him a pint at the bar, where we caught up with each other and gossiped about the relatives around us. He asked about Carla who he considered the prettiest girl in the room. She came across when she saw us watching her, and I thought it was nice the way she and him got along.

The hustle of the Reception played itself out. Carla and I sat near open French windows, where she said she wanted to talk with my father again later, and she asked about other faces in the gathering.

'Well, that guy there is the famous one in the family.

He went off the Weakest Link in the first round. He had an "either or" question and said pass.'

'And the big bald guy there, with all the bling?'

'Cousin Rod. Used to be a drug dealer.'

'Oh.'

A middle-aged couple, very much *Keeping Up Appearances* in loud flowery dress and tweed suit with pork pie hat, entered via the French windows. Auntie Joan recognised me. Carla and I were shocked that she seemed to have a broken nose (taped over) with bruising and two black eyes.

'Have you been mugged, Auntie Joan?' I asked.

'No, no, Alex. It was this silly sod,' she said, indicating henpecked Uncle Ken. 'He picked me up from the shops the other day. "Your door's not shut" he says as we pull away, so I open it to close it properly and he goes and turns right. There's me, bouncing off the tarmac arse above tit.'

That had Carla in hysterics and I was laughing as I clasped Auntie Joan's hand as she moved off, and then shook Uncle Ken's hand.

'What are you doing?' I playfully asked Carla, who was trying to control herself. 'You're a disgrace.'

'That's so funny,' she gagged.

Then we both laughed together until she had to stop tears of laughter spoiling her make-up. She gradually calmed down again.

'Who's that over there?' she asked.

It was a car crash moment where everything seemed to move slowly. I saw the bare shoulders first with the thin straps of a purplish dress, her brown hair short and tousled, her features sharp as she talked in different directions, one hand holding a drink, the other holding that cretin's hand.

I didn't look at him, just the hint of spiky blond hair in the peripheral identified him to me. I felt Carla leaning closer. How could I explain who it was?

She was stunning, Chloe Green, and it was stunning that she was there. I knew the towns north of Manchester went in a lot for inbreeding but I could not have dreamt any connection to the Bride's side.

'An ex-girlfriend,' I finally said to Carla.

I realised she was holding my hands.

'Oh, is it going to be awkward?'

I snapped out of the mesmerising vision that was Chloe.

'No, don't worry about it.'

I believe the meal was excellent, although I only picked at my food. The speeches seemed to go down well due to the Best Man being a wittier wide boy than Warren, and the Bride's side seemed quite articulate.

Chloe knew I would be there. Although she behaved normally she must have clocked me as early as possible. I watched her across the room. She carried herself with the class and deportment of most wedding guests who are dressed in their finest and enjoying an occasion, but in her laughter and flirty behaviour with that cretin next to her it was clear she was as unsophisticated as ever. I remembered examples of her crudeness, what she liked, how she screwed. I knew about the tattoo across the small of her back, and about the six-inch scar at the top of her left thigh from where she fell out of a nightclub. I also knew how wonderful she smelt and what it felt like to cuddle up naked in bed while watching snow fall on Christmas morning. She glanced slowly over once. I could not decipher the meaning of her look. Was she thinking something similar to myself; was she apologising, or was she not thinking anything at all? Next to me, Carla laughed at something said on our table.

Later, everyone moved upstairs to drink and dance the night away. I did take to the floor with Carla, but kept leaving her to it with the “clubbers”, then she would come across and drink with me. She was such lovely company that for periods of time I forgot that Chloe was actually in the room, until she moved through my line of vision or I sought her out on the dance floor.

It was as I watched Carla across talking to my dad that Chloe approached me. I gestured for her to sit. She was hot from dancing; she helped herself to my drink as if it were the most natural thing to do. It was a good thirty seconds before either of us spoke, her sitting there fanning herself, me finding her cleavage cruelly fascinating. There was so much I wanted to say to her and yet in the end we just had a quick shallow chat about each other’s circumstances and gave expressions about being cool with everything. And then she was gone with a lingering caress of my cheek back to that cretin.

Carla made me dance again. The loud music and the alcohol made the night hotter so I was glad to escape and sit chatting with my cousins, who included Rod with all the bling. On her visits from the dance floor, a flushed Carla would flop down beside me and say how nice certain people were and what a bad dancer Dale from the Wolves was. During the night she became friendly with cousins Vicky and Carmen from the Stretford branch of the family, as well as chatting with Michelle, probably about my childhood. While I conversed with a cousin about Manchester United, I watched Carla go over for another girlie rendezvous with Vicky and Carmen. Dale from the Wolves joined their party and I saw Carla giggle at something he said. He was very close to her with his floppy mop of hair. I started to compose my "he's big but I can take him" line, but my cousin insisted I paid attention as he reminisced about Eric Cantona. When I glanced back across the crowded room, Carla's face seemed to have dropped, her fingers were pressing against the hem of her dress; Dale from the Wolves made a movement with his head that seemed to suggest their conversation had hit a brick wall and he should be somewhere else. It was Carla who moved off, and I noticed she was immediately happy talking to somebody else, and then my United colleague was up to Ryan Giggs.

Later on, Carla led me back to the floor as it was time for the old smoochies to be played; George Michael and Phyllis Nelson, etc. I remember the fun of moving close with the happy and warm Carla, aware of Michelle and Dale from the Wolves nearby, and Cousin Rod with his woman, and Warren and his new wife, and Chloe and that cretin. The whole event had proven to be much more enjoyable than I expected, Chloe apart. My family had been on their best behaviour.

When we drifted out to our taxis on a calm starry night there was only Carmen from Stretford letting the side down with a crude snogging session with some guy in the doorway, and there was a brief fight on the car park that I steered Carla away from. I kissed Michelle goodnight, Dale from the Wolves gave me a manly handshake, I locked eyes briefly with Chloe and then I was in the taxi with Carla and away.

When we got to my Nan's house she was still up and in her dressing-gown, making sure her house guests had coffee and tea. In the crowded lounge, Carla sat on me, and she took part in the conversation more than I did, while I felt her hand caressing the back of my neck. I was quite merry, pleasantly warm, very happy to be so close to Carla, feeling her body occasionally wiggling to find the most comfortable position. Even though my Nan and three of the girls went up to bed Carla stayed where she was, and we chatted intimately below the general chatter.

'So I'm sharing a bed with a Robateau,' she said.

'Yes, Lucy Robateau. I've always fancied cousin Lucy. It looks like I'm in a sleeping bag down here.'

'Poor you. Would you like me in there with you?'

'Do you have to ask?'

'I could sneak down.'

'So you could.'

'Alex, I've enjoyed being here with you.'

The only other girl remaining went to bed. Cousin Billy farted. A can of beer cracked open.

'What did Dale from the Wolves have to say for

himself?'

'Nothing much.'

If she had not been sat on me I would have missed the miniscule tensing up.

'He wasn't funny with you, was he?'

'Alex, right, shush, it's bed time.'

I was ready to let her go up, just savouring contact with her a little longer, but she took my silence for being concerned for whatever had been said.

'He was just a little out of order,' she said softly. 'It was nothing.'

'What did he say?'

She now decided she was tired. I clamped my hands around her waist.

'Right, well, he was saying something on the lines of... he found that the microscopic hairs on my sexy legs that I'd missed when shaving were worryingly turning him on.'

I looked at Carla's legs before me. It was a line I would have used myself. I had to laugh.

'Don't laugh,' she scolded me, then she whispered, 'What about your sister?'

Cousin Billy farted again. The television channels began to head more down-market. I thought of Dale from the Wolves and my sister as I absent-mindedly caressed Carla's thigh. There was no way his Super League wages would remain in Michelle's life for any length of time.

'Better if you don't come down,' I told Carla. 'It might get a bit squalid down here.'

'Okay, I'll go and find pretty Lucy, then.'

'I'll see you in the morning.'

She kissed me open-mouthed and I let her go up to bed.

TEN

It was gloriously dark blue with Chelsea Football Club emblazoned in white, fluttering atop the flagpole at Kentmere Tennis Club.

'What the bloody hell is that?' asked Nervo, shielding his eyes from the glare as he came up to join me and Tim on the sun terrace, early Saturday morning.

Tim took his time over a massive yawn, before saying, 'Funnily enough, that's exactly what Alex just said. Well, not exactly, it was a bit stronger. We're washing the flag for some reason. He didn't like my choice of replacement. Harry Madox has gone for something else.'

'Well, can you get that down, anyway?'

'Hey, stop being disrespectful. Just because you follow Salford United.'

Harry Madox came bounding up to us with a package under his arm, letting on to Nervo. Tim worked the ropes and a Union Jack flag then went up into the bright morning sky. Nervo began collecting up empty cans, tutting at the gross thoughtlessness, while Tim moved across to chat with Harry, who was the first barman to arrive for work. I stood there with my neck craned, watching the flag slowly start to ripple in the breeze.

Nervo said, 'For you I believe, Alex.'

I shot him a glance, then down to where he was looking. The van with the day's bouncy castle had just pulled in.

'Right, then,' I replied, geeing myself up. 'But you look out for the clown.'

He opened his arms wide, 'Don't I always?'

The car parks were still virtually empty at that time of day, except for the dozen or so break of dawn swimmers. I watched as Tommy Macro stepped from his Jaguar with jacket and briefcase in hand. There was just a casual interest in the Union Jack before he locked the vehicle and headed in. I jogged down through the building, bidding good morning to various staff members who were straggling in. I showed the bouncy castle men where their pitch was, then joined Nervo setting up benches for a barbecue. At both areas on the ground, I found my eyes drawn up to the flag. It would have looked striking anyway; today it totally dominated the building. I wondered at what stage it would be viewed by the person who mattered, and whether I would be people-watching throughout the day. That would be a futile needle in the haystack job and, besides, I would be too busy.

I watched the arrival of the tennis leisure staff, five upper class wasters in their green tracksuits with hold-alls on their shoulders. For athletes they carried themselves with a distinct lack of oomph. Paid twice as much as me, they would organise the day's competitions and paddle back a few balls to the kids. I moved off before I might have to speak to them. I came across Nichola Duckinfield up from the car park, almost tripping as she realised it was me. She looked fine in a white Kappa tracksuit. She dropped her bag and nervously brushed non-existent strands of hair from her right temple, smiling at me.

'Hiya, Alex.'

'Hello. You're here early.'

'Yes, I'm going to use the gym and then get away before the madness starts. I bet you're not looking forward to the day.'

'You could say that.'

'It'll be over before you know it. Then you can sleep all through Sunday, assuming you're not working of course.'

'It's cricket tomorrow.'

'Oh, God, cricket, yes. I had no idea Neil was friendly with your captain. I...'

'Nichola, it's all right. It can't be helped. Are you coming to watch him tomorrow?'

'Well I just might now.'

'I promise not to deliberately run him out.'

She smiled, looking at me. Did her eyes flick over my shoulder to the flag?

'Where's the old man today?'

'He was just here, dropping me off. He's taken my car for its service. He's got a friend in the trade.'

We both found it inappropriate to say anything too personal, now on a busy pathway. She shaped to move off.

'I'll let you get in, Nichola.'

'Thank you, Alex. We'll speak again soon, yeh?'

'Yeah, on a more normal day.'

I was disturbed from watching Nichola's departing backside by the arrival of sour-faced Rachel Calderbank. I decided to stare her down this time, and then a receptionist took my arm.

'You're wanted at the bouncy thing, Alex.'

'The bouncy thing? Are you being saucy?'

She laughed. 'The bouncy castle.'

'Thanks, Kelly.'

On the way, I passed Tina Molina chatting to another woman. Her cheeky smile had me stuttering my stride, unsure whether to stop, settling for a smile back. She looked hot in a pink vestlet and really tight jeans.

At the castle, the first little customers were removing their shoes and Kingy the Clown was making a hat for himself out of balloons to go with his tails and bow tie. The chief Inflatable man indicated for me to look just inside the portcullis. 'Is that yours?'

On inspection, I found a sleeping Tim wedged between the humps in the castle. I gave him a shake and Tim roused himself and rolled out with a philosophical expression.

'Fun, fun, fun day,' he said.

'Looks like it was "fun, fun, fun" all night with Beth.'

'Oh, yes. Now, that's true.'

The morning proceeded to fly by with members and guests streaming in, the tennis courts being the centre of activity, creating a cacophony of noise. The bar staff's contribution was a balloon arch over the sun terrace which was crammed with observers; two of which were the Molinas. Tina was wearing her shades, tenderly holding his hand coming round her shoulder. Mathew's shades were on his head. They looked comfortable and happy, the perfect, affluent couple enjoying a day out together. He kissed her right temple.

Tuohy finally collared me about the flag. I was in a group taking a drinks break on a staff corridor. They all looked on blankly as Tuohy flamboyantly cocked his head up in the direction of the roof.

'It's a film,' said Harry Madox.

Everyone except Tuohy laughed.

'The flag, Alex?'

'It was full of bird shit.'

'This is Kentmere Tennis Club's annual Fun Day, Alex. Would the official Kentmere Tennis Club flag have survived another twelve hours?'

'It was full of bird shit.'

Tuohy left us with a dirty look. Nervo came in through a fire exit. We connected fists.

'You off, mate?' I asked.

'Soon. If that's all right?'

'Of course. Go and enjoy the wedding. I'll walk you out when you're ready.'

Carla ran in from the sun, giving a passing hug to Nervo before collapsing on my legs and taking my lemonade.

'What a day,' she said. 'Harry, have you finished your break yet?'

Harry stood with a wry smile. 'I like the way you wait for me to come and relieve you. That's...'

'Very, very cheeky,' the group called.

I watched Carla for a few minutes, then walked with Nervo down to his car. He rolled down all the windows and took out the Donald Duck sunshield from the dash.

He was reluctant to leave me and Tim, especially for the wedding of a niece he hardly knew. He huffed and got into his warm car. As he prepared to drive out we noticed Karen Hennessy on the other car park. She was staring up at the club as she waited for her child to exit her vehicle. She somehow spotted us and I exchanged cordial smiles. We watched her head in, blonde hair cascading back in a breeze. Macro was there, apparently by chance, welcoming her with pretentious air kisses.

'I could have a woman like that,' Nervo said to me. We laughed and then I waved him off.

A dishevelled naked woman was the first thing I liked to see as soon as I awoke. Failing that, it was a clock. From my position on the sofa I had no idea what time it was, and I knew the throbbing strain behind my eyes would increase if I got up to find out. Being Sunday there was hardly any sound from the street to give me a clue. I would have to stay there and let it annoy me.

The shower started to run, Carla humming an unfamiliar tune. I snoozed away to the comforting noise, glad she was still there, my mind drifting around the previous night with us staggering in from that manic Fun Day. She had made us her version of Beef Stroganoff before we crashed on pillows outside, talking very intermittently.

'Guess who's pregnant,' she said.

'You?'

'Don't be stupid. Francine Moore.' I was none the wiser. 'Reception. Make-up like she's been beaten up.'

'That would have been interesting if it was you.'

'I'm never having a baby.'

'Why not?'

'Oh, my mum's horror story about being in labour with me. I wouldn't come out. I was lazy.'

'Not changed there, then.'

She tutted. 'More wine. Go.'

I obliged. It was seven o'clock in the evening with smoky black clouds diluting the sun, with the temperature falling off rapidly, so I brought a blanket with the bottle and invited her over to share my pillow. She lay back on me and covered our legs.

We seemed to stay there for hours. I played with her hair and snuggled up to her neck and ears. When she started talking about something, I listened, and when she asked me a question, I answered. Really I was thinking about my decision, in truth made immediately after reading that bastard letter, but it had needed to work its way through my system, to be digested somewhere outside my conscious thoughts. I'd gone back in my memory to torching my girlfriend's father's Jag at sixteen, the Ardwick Post Office raid at seventeen, being paid to have a good go at breaking a Bookie's legs with a hammer at nineteen, all done with No Fear. All well thought about beforehand and carried through with force. What could I not do? Yet here I was with adrenalin making my legs shake against this young girl under the blanket. What could I not do? She was rubbing them. It was too easy to turn down. I just had to go back to those times. Think it through, carry it through. Easy.

Carla had started to worry, suggesting we go inside, thinking I was ill or something.

'It's just fatigue and losing the sun,' I said to her. 'A little longer, I'm comfortable, really.'

Carla was hanging over me in a robe and a towel on her head, smelling clean. 'Do you know what time it is?' she asked. 'Get up, it's cricket in an hour.'

She made me brunch of dry scrambled eggs on burnt toast, then we got ready and gathered my gear. We took both cars to the Delaney school, as she was on shift straight after, and were last to arrive. Everything was set, the boundary rope was down before a sprinkling of spectators, the pitch had been rolled and we had a white-coated umpire doing that slow umpire walk while Captain Phillips had his team in a stretching circle.

I jogged over, looking to join Tim, but it was Neil Duckinfield who saw me arrive and made a space for me. We exchanged nods.

'I was on stand-by to keep wicket,' Duckinfield said. 'Now I'm back to twelfth man.'

'Sorry about that.'

The team-talk passed me by. I strapped on my pads and slipped on my inner gloves and then my catching gloves, starting to smack a cricket ball from hand to hand. Tim shared a good luck hug with chief cheerleader Beth over with the home support, before joining me.

'Hiya, Tim.'

'You all right?'

'Yeah, why wouldn't I be?'

'We're batting first.'

'Oh, right.'

The away team trotted from the changing shack and were roundly booed by Beth, Carla and friends.

'Come on!' screamed Beth. 'You can beat this shit.'

'That's my girl,' laughed Tim.

I had to giggle. I allowed my friend to lead me off the field, removing my pads on the way. I sat down on the grass with Carla, saying hello to the usual gang, most there to spend the afternoon drinking. Beth's friend from the violent night out was there, with her phone, but also with a cool-box. She beckoned me to have a rummage and I chose a cola ice pop. I thanked her and settled back to watch Tony Phillips and a team-mate I knew as Ted go out to open the batting.

'Come on, Teddy!' suddenly erupted out of Beth's morose friend.

The shock of it almost led to suffocation for me and Carla as we tried not to laugh. Tony and Ted progressed well.

'Shot, Teddy!' from Beth's friend.

Knowing I was batting at No.6, I was very comfortable in contact with a prostrate Carla, and my lack of sleep was taking me through the rollercoaster of dopiness followed by a pleasant high, no doubt aided by Tim and a couple of mates on the Draw.

'Way to go, Teddy!'

A roar went up from the away crowd as Ted was comprehensively bowled for twenty-four.

'You're shit, Teddy!'

Tim was up like a gladiator. Beth applauded him off.

'I may be some time,' he said.

A ten minute thrash later he was back with 8 to his name. When the score reached 89 it was my turn up to bat. I liked the way Carla deliberately busied herself in the cool-box, then when I was run out for 6 she acted as if I had never been away. I tickled her without mercy. When we had finished laughing and rolling about I sat up to see Nichola Duckinfield arrive to be with her husband. Our gaze was broken by Tony Phillips swearing at the fall of another wicket, and before very long the innings was over.

I got ready for real, aided by Tim throwing the ball into my gloves from various distances. The away team's opening batsmen were fresh-faced and popular with their supporters. They proved to be very talented as well, smacking Teddy and Tim all over the field. Captain Phillips was starting to turn purple. After five overs he brought himself on to bowl, gentle left arm leg-breaks with me up to the stumps. The first delivery went for six over Tim at long leg. The second I took very well. The third took a wicked deflection off a flashing edge straight up into my face. Blood splashed up into my right eye from a gash on my cheekbone. The pain was almost unbearable but I stood it well and refused to fall over. There came a collective "ooh" from the crowd, followed by brief silence as team-mates rushed in; then there came a lone female cackle of laughter from within the away support. It was playfully un-malicious, with everyone joining in as it was clear I had suffered no permanent damage. I felt pats on my back and the batsman expressing concern. The umpire brought a towel for me to stem the bleeding. I said I was okay. Though feeling a little nauseous, my radar had locked on to where the laugh had come from and I sought her out over the towel. I took the knock in good spirit and was looking not to accuse but to share her cheek. Now I wanted to sit down as I recognised the one and only Joely from Mrs B's shop. She was standing arms crossed with a wry expression, amazing on the eye even from several metres away.

'I bet that hurt,' said Tim.

'A bit.'

As Tim led me off the field I stared at Joely, until Carla took me in hand and sat me down.

'Let me see,' she said. 'Oh, I bet that hurts.'

The bleeding stopped and the swelling started. Carla prepared an ice pack from the cool-box as I acknowledged a squeeze on the shoulder from my replacement Neil Duckinfield. I flashed a glance to Nichola, her knees up to her chest and watching with frustrated concern.

Carla asked, 'Does your cheekbone feel broken?'

'I don't know. I can't feel it now.'

'You'd better go to hospital.'

'Oh, come on, surely not. I can't be doing with the hospital again.'

'You might have concussion.'

'I'll just rest here 'til the game ends. Then we'll decide.'

I allowed myself to be nursed by Carla, who stripped off my pads and gloves. I lay back and relaxed with the makeshift ice pack. As the blue sky engulfed me I listened to Nichola talking to someone and felt Carla removing my trainers for some reason.

Joely was over there. She was just across that field. How bizarre.

'Fuck.'

'Does it hurt?'

I started laughing. 'Fuck.'

Carla laughed and flopped her hands on my quivering stomach.

'Has the knock given you Tourette's Syndrome?'

That had me laughing even harder. I sat up and wrestled with her until she protested about my injury and I remembered Nichola being only ten feet away.

I looked away, and found myself focussing on the flag on top of the main school building, so looked away from that as well. I created a blind spot for the away crowd and tried not to listen to them, giving all my attention to Carla. Oh my God, Joely was just over there. The day after changing the Kentmere flag she was sitting just over there. I felt Carla rocking against me as something comical happened out in the middle and looked at her and we shared a smile. Oh my God, I just lay back down and returned my attention to the sky.

I could hear the two opening bats still pissing on our bowling. Carla sank to my level for a fresh appraisal of my facial damage.

'I've just realised,' I said. 'We're really crap.'

'I know you are.'

It was solely because of the presence of Carla that I allowed myself to settle into a pleasant afternoon watching the cricket. I had a beer and kept tending to my face. The cut was small and the swelling not too extensive.

'When do you need to get off?' I asked Carla without intending a second meaning, and not having it register.

'Now, if you're going to be all right.'

'Yeah, don't worry. I'll show you my shiner tomorrow.'

Carla gathered her things, kissed my good cheek and left for the club. I watched her go, then leant back to Beth's friend, indicating the cool-box. 'What else have you got in there?'

'Feel free.'

I chose a fancy Cappuccino dessert.

'Spoon?' I asked with cheek. The girl came up with a teaspoon. 'You should think about taking up outside catering.'

Now there was just the slightest tetchiness in her eyes. I took my dessert for a bare-foot wander away from the home support. With my numb face I could not smile as Tim finally took a wicket. I looked to where Nichola had met an old acquaintance together with baby. I walked the boundary rope into opposition territory. They were a well-to-do crew in designer gear with nice cars parked in the background. Bottles were being bandied about.

I watched her rise from the crowd, long legs in jeans taking forever to lever her thin frame upright. Her hair in those bunches again. Her bosom tightly defined in Lee Cooper white tee-shirt. With hands in back pockets, she moved to a rendezvous point.

ELEVEN

I was quite taken with Joely's sexy walk towards me, barefoot over the parched grass. She was pretending to be serious as the gap slowly closed between us.

'Well?' she asked.

'Sorry?' I said without moving my lips.

'What took you so long?'

'I was counting my teeth.'

She was make-up free and I realised that her skin was even purer than Beth's. There was amusement behind those full lips.

'You're always beat up. Last time we met, you had facial damage.'

'Yeah, about that, sorry I was a bit rude. It was a really bad time.'

'It's all right. I got over it.'

I slotted easily into staring at her again. Finally she motioned for me to speak.

'It's just, you, you say such sarky things but without any hint of bitchiness. It's just unusual, that's all. Anyway, good team. Are you with a particular player?'

'Now you think I'm a groupie?' She smiled. 'Was that bitchy? Actually, I'm just with a friend, watching her brother. He's the one who hit you in the mush. Your girlfriend seems very nice.'

'Carla? Just a friend. Just a good friend.'

Distant police sirens briefly disturbed us.

'Are we coming or going?' she asked.

'What do you mean?'

'Well, are you going to invite me to your crowd or do you want to come to mine?'

I imagined Nichola Duckinfield looking at me like I was some kind of male slag. 'My gang are a miserable bunch, so let's go to yours.'

'Okay. We've got some tasty chicken.'

'Picnic! Great.'

We did the half-sideways slow walk, mutually attentive. I desperately wanted to pull on her bunches, and overdosed on all the different facets of her youthful beauty. There was also the subtle perfume I had liked so much in Mrs B's shop. Getting nearer to the boys in her group (with one completing a tale "...so I was just cacking myself when it happened", and then laughing like a hyena) she realised I was aware she was deep in thought about me, so came out of it with a smile.

'I liked the way you were run out. It was very comical.'

Before I could play-act at being offended we were both stopped dead by the sight of a scruffily dressed pot-bellied man with a flowing mullet of a hairstyle running from left to right across the field. Then, out of the shrubbery, dashed a line of three policemen. The procession went right through the game, nobody apparently willing to rugby tackle the fugitive, and then they were gone off the other side of the grounds. Although it hurt like hell, I was in hysterics and Joely laughed with me.

We staggered to her friends who were all agog at the

incident. We sat down facing each other, her legs crossed in a cute manner. Somebody cracked a joke about a Benny Hill sketch and we fell into each other laughing.

I had my chicken, Joely and I eating close and intimate. The surreal police chase had broken what had been thin ice. I watched her sexy mouth ravage the white meat, fascinated, part of me trying to be normal with her but also thrilled at how relaxed we were together. What was normal at the moment anyway? Who was this girl? All I knew was that she was beyond gorgeous, carried no airs that came with being beyond gorgeous, and had enough about her not to hold a grudge after being so rudely insulted.

'I hope he got away,' she said.

'So do I.'

As we sat there I accepted defeat with the grace of an England player. When all the sporting pleasantries were completed I had to choose between Tim, Beth and Beth's friend, or staying with Joely.

'No, you take care of them, Timmy. I'll see you tomorrow.'

I turned back to Joely who was saying goodbye to her friend. Joely offered me a small plaster, then put it on me by invitation.

'So what now?' she asked. 'Shouldn't you have dumped me by now?'

We found the nearest pub garden and absolutely delighted the Landlord with our consumption of two glasses of orange juice, just enjoying talking until the dipping sun annoyingly lined up with my eyes. The chat had been in general, neither of us wanting to go into too much personal detail, it was enough to be in each other's company, with it transpiring that she disliked going to "Uni" as much as I disliked cutting grass. She hated Man United as much as I hated Man City. The glass-collecting Landlord despised the pair of us.

'Let's get out of here,' she suggested.

'Where would you like to go?'

'I thought you could take me back to your caravan.'

I led the way to my Audi, with a little bump of the hips for her cheek.

On the drive to my village there was one thing concerning me. Not whether she would look down her perfect nose at the flat above the Takeaway, because she clearly was not that type of person. I liked it there above Mike Yu's, the village was lovely, it suited me. I just wished I lived in a more conventional apartment; one that said to Joely that I was at least making progress like a normal adult and not somebody one pay cheque away from the Big Issue.

She had changed the music channel and was settling down into the passenger seat. I was surprised when she rested her hand on my thigh. I tried not to think too much into this gentle action but on the quiet I found it staggering. I glanced across as she felt my muscle during a gear change. Could I take a route that would give the clutch a hammering? Watch the road, Alex.

In the end she ran up the stairs like it was an adventure playground, pausing to enjoy the view of sunbathed countryside and red sky.

'What a cool place.'

'You like it? Make yourself at home while I shower.'

Being a student, she went straight to the fridge, helping herself to a chunk of cheese, then wandered around inspecting everything. She moved aside the black curtain near to the door probably expecting to find a south facing window. Instead she got brickwork, then there was the mat below it, a type not seen since infant school.

I left her to it and had a quick but thorough shower. While giving my teeth a brushing a Hygienist would approve of I stared at myself in the mirror. She was there in my flat. She was there in my flat and the flag was changed. I dispensed with the sodden little plaster and let the cut breathe. I heard her messing with the radio channels and then recognised the classical tune coming under the door from an advert and liked it very much. In just a towel I padded through to my bedroom, stopping as she was pointing down at the mat.

'Should I be worried about this?'

'Errm, I have got an explanation for that. In a minute.'

When I came out in my grey sweats she was all giddy.

'I know! I know! You rent it out to the local tramps.'

That amused her and we were laughing and cuddling. Now the cricket match and meeting her again was all a blur. I could not believe I was holding her, and could not believe the buzz she caused inside my chest.

'Well?' she asked. 'Explain the mat.'

I paused for effect.

'I practise catching a ball thrown off the other wall.'

'Doesn't the banging annoy your neighbours?'

'She's under the impression it's the plumbing.'

Joely laughed as she went to play pool, surprising me by actually being able to hold the cue. She almost cleared the table.

'What do you think of that?'

'I think you're better at pool than me.'

'I'm better at cricket than you.'

She went back to the fridge, taking my last Crunchie.

'Typical student,' I said.

'Yep, that's me.'

She jumped onto the sofa and I joined her. For a moment I enjoyed staring at her profile, then had the strange thought that she might be thinking I was watching her devour the phallic confectionery.

'So, tell me what you're studying.'

'Oh, please, no.' She put on the TV. 'I'm starting to hate it. Let's not talk about that today. I think it's cool here, it's got a nice atmosphere.'

I smiled as raised voices came from next door. A man, probably Miss Brocklebank's devoted boyfriend, said something on the lines of "speak to me like that again and I'll fucking knock you out."

My next question was lost as she shuffled up to me, freed her hair and stroked it downwards. That fresh mouth opened slightly. She briefly assessed my facial injury.

'I'm not being deliberately evasive,' she said.

'It's all right. I don't think you go to "Uni". You work at McDonald's, don't you?'

'Maybe. Then again I might be an illegal immigrant.'

'No, you're not. I've had one of those already, anyway. That is, to say, not that I'm going to be having you.'

'Are you not?'

She folded her long legs into an impressive yoga position, with me so close and showing great restraint in not touching her. Suddenly I was finding it difficult to stay calm, which I found confusing after our relaxed meeting. Part of me was looking for an excuse to get up and move away from her. Joely remained quiet, listening to the radio.

'Have you any plans tonight?' she asked.

'No.'

'Good. So I can hang out here as long as I want.'

Finally I sensed that she was aware of my unease and made a conscious effort to shape up, pulling the laces of her trainers free. 'I did say for you to make yourself at home.'

She kicked off the shoes.

'Well, that's a start,' I joked with a lewd tone.

She took mock offence and then flopped back on the sofa, looking through satellite channels. Something excited her, 'Oh, oh, Time Team, Time Team.'

'You don't like this, do you?'

'It's great. Unearthing the past.'

'Jesus, let's open another trench.'

The early evening moved happily along, accompanied by her choice of Westlife CD (not mine – previously obtained by the shoplifting ex-girlfriend from Watford). The student had found the wine in the bottom of the fridge and gone to stand barefoot outside the door with the dark sun huge and low in the cloudless sky. I started cooking my perfect quarter-pounder burgers that would sit in toasted sesame seed baps with just the right amount of ketchup and mustard. The thought of Carla's dodgy burgers the other night sent a wave of guilty betrayal through me which I quickly shrugged off as I leaned away from the steam of my George Foreman grill to look at my guest.

'Do you want cheese?' I called.

'Of course I want cheese.'

After she finished speaking, her profile turned away and her hair swished around. I visualised her in the shower, squeezing wet hair down her neck, her shoulder blades taut and her lower back all sleek.

'Alex.'

'Yes, dear?'

'You've got a visitor.'

TWELVE

I froze at my position in the kitchen, opened up the grill, then silently swore, deciding it must be one of my lady friends. I would try to keep it down to an awkward ten minutes. I showed my face, surprised that Joely was giving me a happy smile. At the bottom of the steps stood little Rachel Yu, shyly staring up at the woman she didn't know. On seeing me, her face lit up. I held Joely from behind, something she naturally moulded into.

'Yes?' I called down to the girl. 'Is there something you want?' Rachel nodded. 'Well, come up, then.'

The little girl ran up and stopped at Joely, who dropped down to her level while I made the introductions.

'It's very nice to meet you, Rachel,' said Joely, with a smile.

I went back to the burgers while Joely found some blackcurrant juice for her new friend.

'What's wrong, Rachel?' I asked.

'I didn't like my tea.'

'What did you have?'

'Chicken that was pink.'

'Urrgh. Do you want one of my super burgers?'

She nodded. 'I saw you the other day.'

'Did you, where?'

'You drove past me and my Auntie in your car.'

'Was I with two beautiful blonde women?'

'No.'

'Wasn't me, then.'

We had the food outside, with Rachel making sure she sat between us, never taking her eyes off Joely. Then with the charming innocence of childhood she leant over to whisper into my ear, 'She's the nicest.'

I replied, 'I know.'

Excluded from the secret, Joely happily smiled at me.

Half of Mike Yu's head appeared looking for his daughter.

'She's here, Mike.'

'Okay, Alex.' Then he saw Joely and seemed to go up on his tiptoes. 'Now, who's this delightful young lady?'

'Mike, this is my friend, Joely.'

'It's a pleasure, my dear.' Then he disappeared, singing, 'Joely, Joely, Joeleee, Joeleee,' to the Dolly Parton song *Jolene*.

There was no help with the washing-up, instead the girls stayed outside talking about Rachel's school and pop music. I eavesdropped for anything personal from Joely. The call to leave came from Mike Yu, Rachel politely saying goodbye to her new friend, then running in to hug me.

I came outside. Joely watched Rachel leave.

'How sweet is she?' asked Joely.

'I'm making coffee. Do you want some? Do you drink coffee? It's not a secret, is it?'

'No, it's not a secret. Thank you, coffee's good.' She followed me back inside to sit on the counter. 'So what would you like to know?'

'Do you take sugar?'

'I'm twenty-one, I was born in Johannesburg and that's no connection to my name. I'm studying...'

I stopped her by stepping between her legs to be embraced.

'Alex, I tell you all about me, you tell me all about you, we have sex and then go into reverse.'

'I'm sorry. I didn't mean to spoil your mystery tour. Maybe I'm just in a rush to know you before you start to go off me.'

'Why would I do that?'

I touched a fingertip to her quizzical eyebrows, then went back to the percolator.

'I'll bring your coffee out to the veranda, Miss... What's your surname?'

'Questions!'

She hit my chest and headed back outside. I came to serve her coffee as a train went through. Joely held on to me for dear life.

'Oh, my God. That was frightening.'

I laughed as I settled down close to her, my legs clasped until she felt the air and sound stabilise.

'Joely, is it embarrassing?'

'Is what embarrassing?'

'Your surname. Joely Shufflebottom. Bracegirdle. Pratt.'

'You cheeky get, I've got a friend called Pratt.'

'Sorry.'

We relaxed there enjoying our drinks, Mrs B briefly heard gossiping to somebody, but I chose not to identify her. It led me to think back to seeing Joely as the beautiful stranger in the street. I vowed never to hate her again, even when she would be inevitably cruel to me. She was watching me carefully. Yes you will, I thought.

She suddenly asked, 'What's your surname?'

'Questions from Joely. I'll tell you mine if you tell me yours.'

'Go on, then.'

'Robateau.'

'Rubber Toe!?' She almost fell off her seat with laughing. I half started to go into the French Canadian origin but her hilarity beat me down. 'Rubber Toe!?'

Coldplay took the late shift on the music front. She had asked to stay the night while I was still pondering whether to suggest it or not.

'Would you like to change into something?'

'Why?'

'Errm, no reason. Fine.'

I had lost track of time lying together there on the sofa. Normally Sunday evening television would have been given a wide berth but I happily watched the easy banality of it. She was following some James Nesbitt drama but remained attentive to me throughout, enjoying the closeness just as much, occasionally talking, shifting position, pushing her bum back into me.

I reclined in an almost dreamlike state, feeling her warm torso through the tee-shirt, her little feet now wriggling against my own. I seriously wanted for nothing else in the world. Would it be possible to fall asleep there?

No, she should have my bed. What about the sheets and towels? It had not entered my mind to seek to make love to her. She laughed at an advert on the television, stirring me, starting to get up until she stopped me.

'Don't go.'

'I was just going to prepare the room.'

'It'll be fine.'

'Shouldn't you call someone, if you're staying here?'

Why ask that? I wondered.

She sat up and half turned. 'I suppose you're right. I'll just call my boyfriend.' She watched my face freeze for three seconds before laughing and jumping to her feet. 'Come on, Rubber Toe. I want to annoy the neighbours.'

'Why, are you a bit of a screamer?'

She pretended to be offended. 'I want to play ball.'

'You can't be serious?'

'Of course I am.'

She skipped over to the mat and flopped down with her feet splayed out, examining the ball. I joined her and took my directed place behind. With the gloves on, she had her first throw, but it was so soft it bounced twice on the way back.

'How girly is that?' I asked.

'You throw, I'll catch.'

I took it steady, she collected the ball with excited yelps. Gradually I did the competitive male thing and built up the power until she was recoiling and struggling to catch cleanly, and then one went through to the curtain and we collapsed down to the mat laughing.

'Well, I've never done this before,' she said, catching

her breath.

'You'll expect it every time.'

'I can't move now.'

'You don't have to. This is where you're sleeping.'

'Aaargh!'

She gave me a few smacks around the chest.

'What's this?' I laughed. 'You're like Grace Jones slapping Russell Harty.'

That baffled her. She lashed out a couple more times before succumbing to my weight with a girly giggle. We both saw the clichéd situation unfolding but the first kiss when it came was still slow and wonderful.

Joely had woken while I was still asleep, probably due to the curtains failing completely to keep out the sun. She had showered, and then wearing one of my tee-shirts tucked into her jeans had taken a walk for a paper, encountering Mike Yu on the way back, 'You get the lazy bugger up,' he said.

I had breakfast on the go when she came in.

'Bacon and eggs do you?'

'That'll be lovely.'

'How do you like your eggs? Over easy? Sunny side up?'

We smiled because both of us had no idea what I was talking about.

'Fried would be good.'

She joined me, hands in back pockets, trying to buy a kiss. I cracked the eggs in a flamboyant Ready Steady Cook fashion before obliging.

‘Did you think I’d done a runner?’

‘Not at all, no. No. I saw you down the street.’

‘I’ve got some bad news.’

‘What bad news?’

‘The pottery store lady’s having terrible trouble with her leg.’

‘Did you know, there was a time I thought she was related to you.’

‘Oh, thanks.’

She left me with a pouty kiss to go settle down outside. I served the fry-up, sitting down facing her.

‘What?’ I asked, noticing the hesitant way she accepted her plate.

‘Am I treading on someone’s toes being here?’

‘No. Why?’

‘Your friend from the cricket was here.’

‘Carla? Was she now?’

‘Yes, gave me a right dirty look and backed away down the alleyway.’

Joely flinched as a train passed through. I thought it a welcome sound for a change. We both tucked into the breakfast in silence for a few minutes. I wondered why Carla didn’t just say “sorry, didn’t know Alex had a visitor, I’ll catch him some other time.”

‘When are you next free?’ I asked Joely.

‘Why?’

‘I thought we could do something together.’

‘You mean go on a proper first date? Now, that would be nice.’ She watched me hacking through my tough bacon. ‘Ask me, then.’

'Joely... Can I take you out sometime?'

'Is that it?'

I was laughing. 'What do you want, flowers?'

'Oh, you're magic, you are.'

I got up with my last sausage in my teeth, leaving her with a Tommy Cooper: 'Juslikethat!'

'What!?' she called.

'My God. Tommy Cooper, no? You've had a deprived childhood.'

I brewed up, then she was there with her plate, preparing to depart.

'You're going?' I asked. 'I thought we could have the first date now.'

She took me into a leisurely embrace.

'I wish I could stay. I've got things to do. Will you call me a cab?'

'I'll drive you.'

'No, let me get a cab.'

It was fifteen minutes before the triple blast of the minicab's horn disturbed our dreamy smooching. She kissed me with great deliberation and led me by the hand down and around to the front. The large, gum-chewing, shaven-headed taxi driver nodded at me with warm familiarity and then looked at Joely's figure.

'I'm free tomorrow night,' she told me.

'Tomorrow night, then. Your number, I haven't got your number.'

She flapped, turning to the driver through his open window. 'Have you got a pen, mate?'

He obliged and I watched her delicate fingers scrawl

her phone number on the back of my hand. Then I had to let her go. She tried to get her window down but the driver was not the most romantic of souls as he sped away.

Pedestrians passed me as I stood there trying to permanently picture Joely on my brain. It was just like the first time I'd seen her: a strange sort of guilt or feeling of being unworthy that had me flitting from beautiful eyes, to her skin, to her hair, but unable to create the full image and desperately frustrated that she was gone. I shared an acknowledgement of the eyes with hairdresser Janet who was arriving on her bike. Mrs B was out of position.

Before I knew it I was climbing the stairs, pondering where to take her the following night. I looked at the telephone number on my hand, suddenly panicked at the thought that they might be a random selection, that she would not be coming back and Tuesday night would now be horrible. No, it wouldn't be like that, it would be special and memorable. But where to go? Would she want to do something unusual or the regulation Pictures and a meal? Coming in out of the sun it took a second or two to make out that there was a grey shape sitting in my flat.

THIRTEEN

My eyes finally identified the grey shape sitting in my flat.

'Jesus, Mike, you gave me a start there.'

I carried on, merrily thinking about Joely, before realising that Mike Yu had never invited himself into my flat and never looked that serious before. He was drawing a brown package forward between his feet. It was in one of his takeaway bags. I felt my heart seem to empty and went fractionally weak in the legs. I think I briefly put my hands on my hips, then rubbed my chin, and then, because it was there, I sat on my pool table, aware that Mike was talking sternly, but the words at first passed me by. I strained to take control of my facial expression again, seeking out Mike who had started to pace the room.

' "Mr Yu, you will give this to Alex Robateau unopened," said the big ugly man in the suit. Not "would you mind" but "you will". I don't like people approaching me like that. What is this, Alex? What's in this?'

'When did this happen?'

'Just now. In front of my daughter.'

'I'm sorry, Mike. It's... something and nothing.'

'And how did he know I was Mr Yu?'

I looked at the bag on the floor. Maybe Mike thought it was drugs.

'Your name's above the shop, Mike.'

'I didn't like it.'

'I know you didn't.' I jumped to my feet, with the shock now dispersed. I had known it was to come through Mike Yu, and now that man's part was played out, I just had to get him out of the flat with the minimum of fuss. 'I'm sorry, Mike. I promise nobody will bother you again.'

'Are you in trouble, Alex? Because if you are I'll call my brother.'

'No, Mike. Everything's fine. Again, I'm sorry.'

Mike allowed himself to be ushered out, lingering for an explanation, but I had no intention of spinning a tale and was glad to get the door closed and listen to Mike go downstairs.

Now I was left alone with the package, watching it, expecting it to move or start ticking. I felt hot around the temples. There was no noise. That's what I was aware of. I wanted the sound of traffic or trains, but there was absolutely nothing to disturb this.

I went to the mat with the package sitting there on the floor in front of me. I had every intention of opening it very soon, after the next catch, or the next.

The gloves came off and I started to pick at the Sellotape™ holding it together. I became incredibly excited as wads of cash began flopping out, but it was a very unhappy excitement. It was business. It was not a feeling of bonanza, although that amount of money brought its own obscene fascination. I would count it, but at some other stage. A newspaper cutting came out onto the floor, from a local free paper and the story was about a road safety campaign or something equally inconsequential. Three residents were pictured and named, with Alan Mathers within the added red circle. He was quite handsome, wispy hair, good smile. I saw there were no dates on the clipping. Now the folded typed note was free. I stretched full length on my front, letting it fall open.

NAME
ALAN MATHERS

AGE
44

ADDRESS
9 THE MOUNT, CANDLESBY

'Candlesby. Fucking hell!' I was up and pacing.

Candlesby was no more than five miles away – a posh little village. I stomped to my bedroom and flung open the curtains, staring out to grey woodland far beyond the Red Lion.

'Mathers!'

Can you hear me over there?

I slowly returned to the fact file, slumping down with my back to the wall.

OCCUPATION
CHARTERED ACCOUNTANT

OCCUPATION ADDRESS
OFFICE ABOVE CHEMIST, HIGH ST, TWICKENHAM

CAR
SAAB CONVERTIBLE, BLUE, (REG) MV59 EER

MAIN HOBBY ADDRESS
EWAN BROOK GOLF CLUB

The money took my eye again. Deep breaths were required. Get up, get out. The bike was taken to ground level and I got away as quickly as possible. I wanted to think and to plan, but all I could focus on was being with Joely. I pumped the pedals, forcing myself to concentrate. It was not really going to be a plan anyway. No need for an alibi. That complication surely only applied when there was a connection to the victim. Besides, plans had a habit of going wrong. It was more a case of gathering basic information, confirming what Mathers looked like now, checking access to his home, watching for a routine at his place of work or his leisure time, and then it might all come down to the time it took to walk up a drive and ring a doorbell.

I realised with a start that I was heading down country lanes towards Candlesby, and so diverted away. Up ahead, a girl walking her dog had the same hair as Joely. I sped past. So no plan then, just opportunity. Do it and forget it. Have nothing, no paperwork, no press clipping, in the flat. Change nothing in your life for a good while. Be normal with everybody. Just secure the money somewhere.

'Jesus Christ!'

My profanity and squealing skid frightened the life out of a couple of elderly walkers. The money. One hundred grand sitting on my living room floor. I headed back as quickly as possible, to scoop it all up, wondering where to stash it. I thought it would make sense to split it into two, but then a hiding place as good as a Swiss safe deposit box came to mind and I kept it all together. First I peeled off five £50 notes. This made me think of the date with Joely. In theory I could take her to Paris for a meal now. I could take her anywhere in the world.

I worked quickly on my knees, counting away, occasionally checking for watermarks, sure that Sod's Law would bring a visitor. The cash was taped up in a plastic bag. The extra fifties were sealed in an envelope and put in my back pocket.

I drove carefully to Kentmere. Turning off the road into the staff car park was done on auto-pilot as the sight that greeted me caused adrenalin to pump violently to the top of my head and cause dizziness, maybe even temporary blindness. There was Dibble everywhere, all over the members' car park: panda cars, vans, fluorescent jackets galore, plain clothes CID, forensics people in their all-encompassing white suits and blue plastic booties. Somehow I managed to park and tried to relax as I watched them all. Immediately it reminded me of several years ago when a mate and I were driving off without paying from petrol stations; then to see two Dibble exiting a panda car outside my house in that lazy, take ages to put on the cap and arrange the paperwork manner. But they were there to visit a neighbour, and this scene on the Kentmere car parks became immediately obvious to be nothing to do with me.

Still fascinated by the gathering, I carried my parcel in

through the main entrance to reception. There were a handful of members milling around. The receptionists were in their little office at the back. The one who Carla had said was pregnant came out chewing a toffee and smiling to me.

'Hiya, Alex.'

'What's going on out there?'

'There was a fight. Then Mrs Johnson left.'

'Mrs Johnson left?'

'Yeah, left in her car, right over Mrs Lloyd. She's been taken to hospital. She might be dead. We might have to close today.'

'God…' I left a respectful pause. 'Anyway, I just wanted a quick word with Libby if she's about.'

'I'll get her for you. Oh!' She was having an idea, moving towards Mathew Molina who I hadn't noticed along the counter, filling out a form of some kind. 'Mr Molina, Alex might be the man. Alex, Mr Molina's missing a partner for a doubles match. Do you fancy it?'

I looked at Molina. Molina looked at me. Stuck-up and piss-poor seemed to pass silently between us.

'I'm useless,' I said.

'Not much better myself,' replied Molina. 'Never mind.'

Libby appeared anyway, wide-eyed and chewing a toffee also. She waved me through.

'What brings you in, Trouble? Have you seen that out there?'

'Yeah, it's mad. Listen, favour, please, Libby. I'm minding some cricket gear for a friend. Can I have a spare locker?'

'I think I can manage that for you. Oh, do you want a chocolate? They're a gift from Gus.' She headed back to the little office to find me a key.

'No thank you,' I called.

She brought the key and a box of expensive looking chocolates to the counter. 'Go on, help yourself.'

I selfishly chose a strawberry one.

'Who's Gus?' I asked.

'You don't know Gus?'

I joked, 'No, that's why I asked.'

'Gus is great.'

I took the new key and jogged to the staff room, luckily avoiding everybody. I found the correct locker, placed my parcel inside, thoroughly checked that it was locked and then backed out. As I did so the locker merged into a hundred others. Then I was quickly out of the building and in my car, watching the crime scene as I left.

I just drove the Audi. The noise from having two windows down cut out the radio, allowing me to relive the brief time spent so far with Joely. It came to me as if in a TV news loop; the fresh beauty near Mrs B's, spying on her with Mike Yu, the strange rejection, the cricket, the evening together, near Mrs B's again. I visualised the police chase at the cricket match.

I went to my flat, cleaned up, ate something, made one phone call, then went on a high speed exodus north again home to Manchester.

I only stopped once and by the time I arrived at the Airport Hilton, by then proudly thinking of Carla at the wedding, I was completely goosed and continued to see motorway at the back of my eyes until I went into the City Centre and out the other side, rising up towards Prestwich with offices and hotels in the mirror. I declined to glance at Strangeways prison on my right. On the start of the main commercial drag into Prestwich I parked up a side road and strolled out to the front. Across the busy road I looked at Deborah's Hair Salon with the good news sprayed on the window that “it's a boy- 7lbs. 7oz”. My sister was working the first chair. She was happily laughing and gossiping away. I entered Deborah's, causing the expected stir of interest in the clientele.

'Hiya, Sis.'

Michelle spun around and her face lit-up in delight. 'Alex!' She grabbed me. 'What are you doing here?'

'I was just passing.'

'Girls.' She turned me. I liked to think the rest of the staff eyed-up the good-looking bloke. 'This is my brother.'

I let on to them all and laughed with Michelle, who pulled me away from her nosy customer.

'Go and sit in the back until I've finished this lady.'

'It's just a flying visit, Sis. I've got some business to do.'

'What kind of business? Nothing dodgy I hope. And what about seeing Dad?'

'I'll come up next month and stay, I promise.'

'Is everything all right with you?'

'Yeah, fine. Listen, I'll shoot off. I'm keeping you from your work.'

'Mrs Stewart's all right, aren't you, Vera?'

'Oh, don't mind me, love. I'm still waiting for my cup of tea.'

Michelle made a face and then cheekily smiled at Mrs Stewart in the mirror. Reluctantly she let me go, giving me another hug before being handed the little envelope from my back pocket.

'What's this?'

'A present,' I said softly. Then I backed out. 'I'll come and stay soon. Goodbye, Ladies.'

I went back into Town. The hotel I had rung earlier in the day was around the corner from Granada Studios with its flagship production Coronation Street making me think of Michelle again, as well as other avid viewers in my extended family. Where I parked bisected the posh front entrance of the hotel and the functional doors to Housekeeping with a trio of plain maids in their cheap striped dresses having a quick smoke. I drifted in their direction, still planning to go in the front way, but then I heard Jimmy Sheridan (Jimmy could always be heard) and the three mingers giggled at the mere presence of one of those natural born jokers in the pack.

'Jesus, what a stink,' cried Jimmy.

As I got closer I could see a pile of dirty laundry bags being sorted by a crouching man with rolled up sleeves of the same material as the mingers.

'Fucking hell,' said the man.

'You look in a bad way there, Jimmy,' said one of the mingers.

'Bad way? It's dreadful, mate. Fucking dreadful.' Jimmy's coarse humour had the mingers and two seated housekeepers all laughing and his face was a picture as he came across a particularly soiled article of clothing.

'Where the hell has this been? Dear me, this is terrible. Talking about terrible, have you seen that new barmaid? I walked through a door into her. I nearly died of shock. Now that is rough. It shouldn't be allowed out in public.'

They all laughed hysterically at him. Suddenly a very large, extremely unattractive barmaid passed through for bar towels. One of the housekeepers tried to gesture Jimmy to be quiet.

'Fucking terrible!' continued Jimmy, starting to turn red. 'Absolutely awful. It should have been put down at birth.' Jimmy started to laugh himself, so wound up was he. 'I've seen some sights in my time but that is fucking horrible.'

Jimmy threw out some full bags for collection, then followed them for a breath of fresh air. Running a hand over his thinning spiky hair he spotted me. His face showed that he was pleased to see an old mate but he didn't say anything, just walked over a flowerbed to offer a very deliberate handshake.

'Go and wait in the bar,' he told me. 'I won't be long. And watch out for Melanie.'

Melanie's flirty eyes spotted new blood as soon as I walked into the green plastic jungle that passed as the bar. I read her silver name badge and politely raised my facial muscles at a handsome blonde in her late twenties. In her youth she would have been stunning, but now I just wanted to ask her if she had been through the entire male staff yet. She made a drink enquiry sound like a come-on. I treated myself on my day out to a beer, disappointing Melanie by moving off with it, away from stiff business types and sitting near one of the miniature glass waterfalls.

Jimmy was quicker than expected, coming into the bar with a lazy carpet-slipper type walk, a Head sports bag over the shoulder of his out-of-date Man' United shirt.

'Can you have a pint in here?' I asked him.

'Can I fuck.'

As we left, Jimmy had a thorough lecherous stare at Melanie.

'Have you?' I asked.

Jimmy considered lying, then laughed. 'Does a grope at the Christmas party count?'

Jimmy had never owned a car, could not drive, and had no intention of ever learning. He rolled a cigarette as I drove us the short distance to Salford, notable only for the view of Old Trafford's stands shining in God's light. We crunched onto broken glass in the middle of a trio of nondescript tower blocks. It was quite cool in the shadows as I locked the Audi and followed, half reluctantly, after Jimmy towards his building with its razor wire above the entrance. We passed a group of girls and boys. The prettiest girl wore a red dress that made her look like a prostitute. She did one of those slow dripping spits that I hadn't seen for a while.

We went up in a lift the size of a telephone box. I refrained from asking Jimmy how he got his furniture up there. I also stopped myself from enquiring what happened to Jimmy's nice house in Stretford. It was good to be in Jimmy's company again, of all the old crew he was the friendliest, but this environment quickly started to drag me down, especially with the slight aroma of piss out on floor ten. Jimmy's flat was on the exposed inner side which was at least clean, with his neighbours showing a liking for flowers. One of them appeared in her doorway, an elderly woman who let on to Jimmy with a smile of three teeth.

The flat was very open plan as the connecting doors were missing for some strange reason. There was a definite woman's touch in the light green furnishings and carpet, with a plethora of Lladro figurines on the shelves.

'Have you got yourself a missus now?' I asked.

'Yeah. Well, somebody else's missus.'

I accepted a can of lager and stepped out onto the small balcony to be faced by a panoramic view of the concrete side of another tower block. 'Lovely view you've got,' I couldn't resist calling.

FOURTEEN

I came back inside Jimmy Sheridan's flat. He was sitting on his sofa watching Sky Sports News, waiting patiently on me. I took an armchair.

'Working with a lot of women, then, Jimmy?'

'They're a bloody nightmare, mate. Listening to them talk about their husbands' problems all day long. It's disgusting. What about you?'

I told him about the tennis club and my area of Surrey. Then we chatted about the whereabouts of old friends, some who were doing well, one who was a bum selling the Big Issue, another a quick-fire father of four.

There suddenly came a manic thrashing about from the flat above, as if someone was having an epileptic fit.

'What the fuck is that?' I asked.

'It's a guy called Jack. He's trying to get through some game on his Playstation 3 without being wounded. It must be fucking frustrating to kill ninety German soldiers and then get winged by a bit of shrapnel. See, it's gone quiet – he's started from the beginning again.'

We watched the sports news for a while, finishing our beers. I felt enormously fatigued, obviously down to the long drive and the drink. My mind was drifting away to Joely when I was asked, 'So, are you seeing anyone?'

'There's someone, yeah. A new someone.'

Joely did not belong there and I was not willing to talk

of her. Jimmy was changing position; I felt he was about to focus the conversation.

'Is Alex in love, then?'

'Love? I don't do that anymore, mate.'

'It's all a load of bollocks.'

Playstation Jack threw himself across the ceiling again and then I could have sworn I heard him growling.

'Yeah, you're right, he's a fucking nutter,' said Jimmy, laughing.

I found it so strange to hear the Jimmy laugh after such a long time. I watched him for a moment, then tried to regain my train of thought. 'What were we talking about?'

'I was saying about sex, it's a load of bollocks.'

'But, if you're with a special person it'll be great forever.'

'You think? I was with Kath Keane for a couple of years, remember her? Quite fit. There I was banging away one day and I suddenly realised I was bored out of my fucking tree. Bored out of my fucking tree.'

'Well...'

Jimmy was up and heading for the kitchen. 'Beer. We need beer. So? What do you need from Uncle Jimmy? What can be so important to come all the way home? Drugs? No. I've heard about some iPhones going cheap.'

I waited for my fresh drink to arrive. It was a Budweiser. Not a brand I particularly liked. I started to drink it.

Jimmy and I came down in the phone box lift. I was

pleased to see that my Audi was still there, although I had to look through a motley gang of youths near the foyer to see it. I counted ten of them, all in various arrangements of baseball caps, hooded tops, cheap trackie bottoms and gold chains. Our passing was noted and there seemed to be a drifting towards a rendezvous point. The two closest to our left side carried the telltale spots of too much speed. I didn't hear exactly what one said to the other, but the use of the word "taxing" was enough to launch me into a fabulous head-butt onto one spotty face. It almost knocked me out. After momentarily being stunned, I realised the flattened youth was a right bleeder as the claret was all over the pair of us. Jimmy had obviously been ready, he was already at the main bunch with both fists up and bouncing like a mad man ready to take on all-comers. There was a quick flurry of punches before I was there beside him to punch a face back into its hood, and then we were at my Audi, in and away.

'There's a McDonald's at the end of this street,' said Jimmy, breathless but calm. 'We'll get you cleaned up and catch a bite to eat, shall we?'

'Christ, Jimmy, is that an everyday occurrence round here now?'

'No, that was very unusual – nobody got stabbed.'

The McDonald's staff who saw us enter decided it was best not to question my bloodied person. After cleaning up in the Gents I was left with just a little bit of pink on my neck and tee-shirt. We ate cheeseburgers and drank coke in silence, both of us doing some people-watching. Then Jimmy stood into the foyer area to make the phone call I'd asked him to make in the flat. He came back in, nodding.

'Oh, right, then,' I said.

'He wants to see you, though.'

I slurped the last of my coke. 'Thought he might.'

We headed back to my car.

'Have you got a jacket?' Jimmy asked as he tugged at my tee-shirt.

My appearance was the last thing on my mind. 'It doesn't matter,' I said.

Following Jimmy's directions we drove for a while and ended up in a nice residential area of Didsbury. 'Park anywhere here,' he said.

Then he led me on foot back along a line of parked cars to a white-washed Victorian villa which was home to a dental surgery. I stopped and looked at Jimmy.

'What the hell's this, Jimmy?'

'Trust me, it's the right place.' He skipped up the steps and rang a bell. 'Come on, Alex, scale and polish.' A pretty receptionist opened the heavy door. 'Hello, we're here to see Keith.'

She indicated for us to go through to the front room and I smiled at her in passing. There were magazines scattered about and a fish tank which held Jimmy's attention until we were joined by a healthcare worker in his white jacket.

'Oh my God,' I said as I suddenly recognised the man as one Keith Jacques, smiling at me and ignoring Jimmy as he came over to embrace me. I couldn't get over the white coat. 'Is this a joke, Keith? How can you be a dentist? It doesn't add up.'

He stepped back to smooth out the fabric. 'I'm not a dentist, mate. You're looking at a newly qualified hygienist.'

He said it as if that was better. I stared at him, bigger than me, fairly good-looking. Every memory of growing up with the man, running wild as teenagers, the crimes and misdemeanours (he led the Ardwick Post Office raid), his natural progression up the ranks with his violent activities to legendary status in certain groups; it failed to fit right then and there in that waiting room.

I just kept staring at him until he shut the door and sat us both down. He was still obviously pleased with me knowing about his upstanding occupation. 'Where've you been?' he asked.

So I told him. While we had our chat, a dentist drill started upstairs, much to Jimmy's nervous discomfort. Keith told me how he was and what had led to his medical training. He was engaged, not to anyone I knew. I settled at last, and then he asked me what I was there for. So I told him. There was no umming and ahhing, no morally intrusive questions, just a knowing nod of the head and a promise to come through for me via Jimmy Sheridan.

We could have reminisced a great deal more but I genuinely felt that Keith was actually busy that day, so Jimmy and I made to leave. Keith shook my hand and again pulled me into an embrace. He ignored Jimmy, then got the door for us. We were almost out onto the step when Keith called me back. He slipped a small clear plastic envelope into my hand. What had he given me, cocaine, or something? I looked down to see about a dozen tiny brushes, like miniature pipe cleaners.

'Look after your gums,' was the last thing Keith Jacques said to me before closing the front door.

The following morning, the Dibble were still at Kentmere, now outnumbered by flowers for the late Mrs Lloyd. The place was still open but very quiet. Extremely tired after my northern excursion, I nevertheless kept myself busy working away from the main building. It was not to think of anything in particular, not the matter at hand or Joely, not even to avoid any awkward scene with Carla. It was just to keep my own council, to enjoy the sun and the work, not paying too much attention to the comings and goings despite the odd shouted party/barbecue/brunch invitation passing between the snobs as they viewed the crime scene.

Close to noon, a Ferrari did catch my eye, the big shiny wheels crunching through to the now overcrowded staff car park, Macro alighting from it. In his sunglasses and open-neck shirt he didn't seem to have the death of Mrs Lloyd hanging too heavily on his mind. He made a bee-line for me. I wiped off some sweat and dirt to face him.

'Morning, Mr Macro.'

'Morning, Alex. Another beautiful day despite all that shit.' He waved a hand in the direction of the Dibble. 'Have we started getting anywhere near busy?'

'Can't say I've noticed.'

Macro let on to passing gym fanatics, allowing me to look at the man. He was a little shorter than myself, blue shirt tucked into tight jeans with ill-matched black shoes, making him look like an off-duty politician. I again wondered if I could take him.

'How's things with you?' Macro asked.

The question was a first to me from Macro.

'Everything's good.'

'So I hear. New girl on the scene?' I gave a cautious nod. 'Tim told me. I was going to call you in yesterday as the precious Nervo went home upset at the road rage incident. But Tim said you'd be with this new bird. Has she got expensive tastes or is she easy to please?'

'Well, we'll find out tonight. First real date.'

'Oh, first date?' He moved off, before coming back, removing his shades. 'Don't take this the wrong way, but would you like to borrow..?' The Ferrari keys were dangling. I had decided once and for all that I could take him. It might be messy but it was guaranteed. The Ferrari: no, I was not offended. Why would I be? The thought of Joely stopped any annoyance at Macro's unusual friendliness. She wouldn't mind if our first date was by bus, but the novelty value was not to be missed.

'I'd like that, Mr Macro.'

'Good. Find me before you clock off today.'

'Will do.'

I watched him go. I decided I was ready for lunch, so headed in. Maybe Tim would be around. Or should I go and seek out Carla? What was I being paranoid about anyway? She probably wouldn't even mention anything about Joely.

On the way in I found myself on collision course with

Tina Molina's cleavage, in its zippered black sports top, bag over shoulder, pink Alice band keeping her hair in check.

'Alex,' she said as if I were a naughty schoolboy. 'You keep bumping into me.'

I had to smile. Only a few weeks ago it would have been a pleasure to flirt with Tina. Now it seemed strange.

'I don't know why I'm going to the gym, I'm bleeding knackered.'

'You're always bleeding knackered. Get the heart going and you'll be fine.'

Normally she would have been touchy feely by then, but she was looking over her shoulder to where I could see Mathew Molina bringing up the rear with his own sports bag.

'Come on, Mathew,' she called.

'Well, don't wait for me, then.' He acknowledged my presence. 'Alex.'

'Mr Molina.'

'Drives me to distraction this woman.'

I politely smiled, letting them pass. Inadvertently I had also stepped aside for Rachel Calderbank and a bar colleague called Grace. Grace nodded at me but Rachel Calderbank just kept up her loud conversation. 'That Gus is a scream. I think he's a friend of Mr Macro's from California. When I met him he was saying to me...'

I wondered who this Gus was, before hearing my name being called. It was Tim, 'Alex!'

'What's up with you?'

'Trouble in the bar. Are you coming?'

Thinking about the death of Mrs Lloyd, I paced Tim up to the club bar, asking what was wrong on the way but he was unclear. We dodged flustered old members to get into the bar, immediately seeing Harry Madox with a bloody mouth facing up to a big man in jeans and Adidas vestlet, aggressively having a silent conversation with himself on some troubling issue. Carla stood there trying to calm the man.

'Carla,' I shouted. 'Come away.'

I moved in, seeing overturned tables and drinks. The big man, and he was big with muscles and tats, seemed to be chewing his tongue and he kept sporadically pointing at me.

'What's wrong, mate?' I asked.

'Eh, fucking what? You, fucking you.'

He kept pointing.

I asked Carla, 'Has he been drinking?'

'Obviously,' she snapped at me for the first time, then cooled. 'But not here.'

'Sir, can I get you a taxi?'

'Eh, I'm gonna fuckin' kill you.' He kept up that annoying pointing. 'Not him, not him, not her, you. Fucking kill you.'

'What's your name, sir?'

'You.'

I glanced at an unimpressed Tim.

'It's going well,' he quipped.

The big man seemed to find a nice bit of tongue to chew on and then his index finger lined up on me again. 'You.'

I thought the situation over. Yes, this guy's going to get the Full Andy Hartson Treatment. I looked at Tim. 'Andy Hartson?'

'Oh, please, yes.'

Andy Hartson was an acquaintance we both knew who had a tried and trusted method for bouncing people out of nightclubs he worked in. Forward I went at speed, left hand grabbing the big man's throat, right hand clamping his balls and he was marched backwards across the bar and slammed through the fire exit doors, down the zigzag ramp and deposited in a heap on a patch of dry mud. I left him gagging and returned to the bar, closing up the doors again. Tim was helping Harry look for his teeth, Carla was not there. I went looking for her, checking the changing rooms and the Ladies. I found her crying on one of the stairwells, immediately taking hold of her, but she just let herself be held and kept her arms crossed.

'He's gone,' I said softly. 'He's gone.'

The crying continued. I moved her hair aside but she turned her head away.

'Carla, baby. It's okay now. He can't bother you again.'

Slowly she calmed and held me back.

I finally met the famous Gus, in the doorway to Macro's office, and I felt silly taking the Ferrari keys under the cheerful gaze of this sun-tanned, sandy haired stranger in an expensive suit with a Rolex on show when he scratched his chin.

'So this is Alex,' said Gus, as if he'd been waiting to meet me. 'Everyone speaks highly of you here at Tommy's club. Well, everyone apart from that woman who runs the bar. I'm Gus, by the way. I'm in the same line of business as Tommy here, only far more successful.' He made me shake his hand. 'I'll give you an option, Alex. Take the Ferrari, or gamble on what I'll lend you for tonight's date.'

He seemed well informed about me. 'I'll risk the Ferrari.'

'Bentley...Continental. But too late. I rest my case. Say no more.'

I juggled the keys as I resisted the urge to do another Andy Hartson.

'I hope she enjoys it,' said Macro from his desk.

I made my excuses and got out into the sun. It briefly crossed my mind to call in on Carla again, but decided against it. Now was the time to focus on Joely. I looked around for the big man I ejected, but the coast was clear. It was better not to have a scene with Macro's pride and joy before even getting it out of the car park. I sat in the Ferrari and took in the interior and fondled the wheel. It was the second time I had been in such a vehicle, although that had been in a less genteel part of the world with unpleasant company. I brought the vehicle slowly out of the car park as I judged the clutch. At the main road I had to stop to let Tina Molina's Chimaera leave. So concentrated had I been on the Ferrari that I had not heard the beast coming alongside. She playacted surprise at the car I was driving, then cheekily laughed and waved as she sped off.

On the drive to my flat I had never experienced such hatred. People stared at me as if I had butchered their entire families to get that car, and nobody let me into traffic. I stopped in front of Mike Yu's Takeaway, ready for some banter with the man, but she was there already. Without waiting for me to call or arrange a meeting place. She was there being served some delicacy over the counter, laughing at something Mike said. Her hair down onto a small black top, flawless bare back, leather pants with silver belt. She turned with a smile. I hopped into the shop and we shared a kiss.

'Hello, Magnum,' she said.

FIFTEEN

I lightly kissed Joely's neck, noticing as I did so that a teenage lad in the queue looked extremely jealous of me.

'What are you doing here?' I asked her. 'I was just about to ring you.'

'Mike's feeding me.'

'Oh, great. Shall we stay here, then? Mike, put us up a table. Hey, Mike, I think she's a student, once you start feeding her it'll be like having a stray dog.'

The lad in the queue found that amusing, but Joely was playfully offended, tugging the front of my tee-shirt. 'Are you calling me a dog?'

'As if I'd do that.'

We stood there in Yu's, seeing so much in each other's eyes. It was beauty and the beast stuff, with my face being full of grime. She found a twig in my hair.

'So, what have you got planned?' she asked.

'It's up the swanney now. It was going to be a nice little Italian.'

'What, a Del Piero? Don't worry, I can eat for England.'

The shuffling queue disturbed the love-in, so I led her out past the Ferrari and up to the flat where she decided to stay outside in the early evening sun. There was more kissing against the railings.

'Where'd you get the car?'

'I borrowed it.'

I found her perfume delicious again. Just kissing her neck became so arousing that I made my move to shower and shave.

We took the Ferrari off into the countryside. Joely again rested her hand on my left thigh, me oddly nervous, glad that little blobs of clouds kept the sun's heat at bay. I felt like sweating again from the day's ingested radiation, plus I was in a permanent state of pre-erection. It was like she was the first female I had been near after a ten-stretch.

The Italian restaurant was a non-descript white property in a modern part of a small Surrey town, but inside it was clean and cosy with red and white checks everywhere and had a welcoming atmosphere. I was pleased it was cool as well. As we were sat I had a good look round at a few couples and a family group. Julio Iglesias provided the background music. Joely placed down her purse and phone and I noticed that of course it was switched off. She went straight for the breadsticks and we laughed together.

'What's your mum like?' I asked. 'I bet she's huge, isn't she?'

'She is not. So, talk to me, then.'

'About what? I'm not allowed to ask you anything meaningful.'

'Have you got any hobbies?'

'Cricket.'

'Oh, we've exhausted that already. I suppose I better tell you what takes up most of my free time.'

'Oh, God,' I sighed. 'You're into something really weird, aren't you? I knew you were too good to be true. It's Naturism, isn't it?'

'No.'

'You keep rats?'

'No. I keep a horse. Called Candy.'

'That's not too bad.'

'I didn't want you to think I was some spoilt little rich girl with a horse.'

An Italian version of Sammy Davis Jnr interjected to take a drinks order.

'Horse riding explains why your lower back's so toned. Stella Artois, please.'

'Bottle, sir?'

'Please.'

'Toned is it?' said Joely. 'White wine, please. You should see my thighs.'

Sammy Davis went away.

'I believe you.'

There was a minute of quiet between us.

'I like men's hands,' she said, taking hold of my right hand. 'I like them big and rough, just like this one.'

'Good.'

'What part of a woman's body do you like?'

'Stand up for me, no, only joking. The area around, between...' I searched for a description. 'Just inside the hipbone, but lower down.'

'Oh, here?' She was rubbing the designated area when Sammy Davis returned with the drinks.

I asked him to give us a few more minutes to consult

the menu.

Close to the Italian restaurant was a small, fairly busy children's play area. Joely led me across and reclined onto a patch of grass.

'I'm stuffed,' she said. 'I still want popcorn at the pictures. What are we going to see?'

I knelt next to her. 'There are only three screens, I'm afraid, so I hope you like my choice.' I brought out a ticket stub for her to look at. It read: Ek Aur Ek Gyara.

She laughed and rolled onto her side to watch the children play. I contented myself with watching the curve of her hip. Would it be a good time to touch it? I was sure she wouldn't mind. I started to ponder on how the rest of the night would pan out. We were expected to sleep together, of course, yet I wanted to wait. I softly touched her side, causing her to turn back and wrap delicate fingers around my forearm.

'Do you like films?' she asked. To my nod she asked, 'What's your favourite film?'

'You've got to be kidding.'

'Favourite film?'

'Impossible. Now if you ask me a favourite genre of film.'

Joely gave me a stern glare. 'Favourite film?'

'Oh, Jesus. Errm, *Platoon*. Have you even heard of it?'

'Of course. Charlie Sheen.'

She rolled back to watch the kids.

'Oh, no you don't,' I said, turning her giggling by her bare waist and then holding her down with my thighs.

'What's your favourite?'

'Well it's between...'

'Sod that!' She screamed with laughter. 'Favourite film, Joely?'

'*Fame*!'

'*Fame*? Fucking *Fame*?'

'It's brilliant.'

'It's all right.'

I tried to recall the School For Performing Arts drama and how it could rate as someone's favourite film. Her laughter subsided. Very strangely for me the "Job" I had taken on suddenly invaded my thoughts and turned me cold. I reached across to Joely's sharp jaw line and then played with those full lips, desire rushing back in, with it the fear that maybe I didn't have as much time as I thought with this girl. I saw her brow crinkle so snapped out of it, having a look down the street.

'Is the car still there?' she asked.

'It is. Do you still want to see a film?'

'Yes, and it had better be the Bollywood thing.'

'I've got tickets for the new George Clooney film.'

'Well, if you insist, then. Are we going?'

She stood and pulled me up, going hand in hand to the car where I got the door for her.

'Thank you, sir.'

I drove slowly through the town, without many pedestrians to stare and only light traffic. We followed a filthy Transit van, Joely giggling and pointing at the writing in the dust, which I had seen many times:

I WISH MY WIFE WAS THIS DIRTY
SHE IS

I took Joely to an old-fashioned cinema with plush red carpets and ornate carvings, a far cry possibly from the out of town multi-plexes she would have been used to. She happily got her popcorn to spite me and that rested between her legs as we watched the movie in the company of about a dozen people.

I found it amusing that the popcorn was gone in no time, and her first numb-bum shuffle had her leaning into me. Joely seemed engrossed in the film, but I became bored with it. I was, however, determined not to sneak glances at her in the half-light. I took hold of her left hand in my own rough mitts, suddenly aware she was looking to see if I intended to place it in my lap. I smiled, maybe she wasn't thinking that at all. There was one little gold ring on the index finger which I gently twiddled around. The nails were immaculate. I took the hand to my lips to softly kiss it, and then the fingers in turn. She was staring now, quite taken aback by such novel behaviour.

It was dark when we came out, joined at the hip.

'Pub?' I suggested.

The little town we were in looked empty on a Tuesday night, so any pubs would be the same. Joely answered with a negative murmur. We found the Ferrari.

'Still here,' I said.

'Whose is it?'

'My boss's.'

'You seriously wouldn't be bothered if it wasn't here,

would you?'

'No.'

There was not a sound out there and the air was warm and still. I came forward and pressed her up against the car and she let out an oomph that flashed me back to rolling around with Carla on the playing fields. Was it too late to consummate that relationship?

'What are you thinking about?' she asked.

I chose my words carefully.

'Making love to you in the back of my boss's car.'

Happy kissing took place.

'Home,' she finally said.

'Okay.'

We drove twenty minutes through blackness before the first road sign appeared. She gave me directions and we eventually returned to some kind of civilisation, coming into the outskirts of a town.

'So you live round here?'

'Left at the next roundabout.'

We passed through a nice suburban area, then an industrial site, then a more rural area with farm building silhouettes. Soon we slowed into another conurbation, two blocks of flats, a lot of housing, more life around with people playing out in the summer evening.

'Down here,' she gestured.

'Okay.'

Even in the sporadic street lighting I recognised Kabul when I saw it. I swerved around rubble, tyres and shopping trolleys. Most houses seemed boarded up, some showing the stars through where their slates used to be.

One of the houses was lit up, with youths and dogs kicking their heels in the front slum.

'This is it,' said Joely. 'Would you like to come in for a drink?'

'Sure.'

I felt like swearing. Yes, I came from a rough area, but fancy living in a total dump like this. But then she was giggling. Realising the joke, I tried to throttle her through her laughter.

'Jesus, Joely, are you trying to get us killed? We're in a Ferrari here, love.'

I did a u-turn, having trouble with the gears which made her laugh even more and I joined in as we made our way back to a normal street three or four miles away. I saw her Citroen, but still asked if it was the right place this time.

'Sort of. I'm staying with a girlfriend tonight. Shopping to be done early in the morning.'

That put the dampers on things for me. I had wanted to be patient on the intimacy front, but now that there was a hurdle I was disappointed.

'You can still come in,' she said. 'Alison's friendly. Not "friendly" friendly, you understand.

'That's a shame.'

'Come on, you.'

Placing my hands on her bare waist, I was led a conga down an overgrown path to the door. Joely stopped suddenly and I shunted into the back of her. With a laugh I looked over her shoulder at the person lingering in the doorway, at first thinking friend Alison was an ugly bird until the features turned into that of a man. Adrenalin exploded inside me, continuing to course my veins even after Joely addressed the man with annoyed familiarity rather than fear.

'Oliver, what are you doing here?'

'To talk,' answered the fair-haired youth. 'I saw your car.'

'We can't keep doing this, Oliver.'

'I'm not stalking you, J. I'm not hanging around Alison's house. I've just got here. Who's this?'

'None of your business. Will you just leave?'

I kept my own council, my heart calming, not seeing a threat from the younger man. Could I have foreseen something like this? What did I expect, that Joely was the Immaculate Girlfriend? Of course she would have an Ex. Joely and I were only together on the slight chance that she was between boyfriends. Oliver seemed like a nice lad, clearly hurting and seeking communication. I could see myself in his position in a couple of months time, and found myself hating Joely again for just a second. Nevertheless, Oliver was about to get the Full Andy Hartson Treatment.

Oliver flounced off down the path. I allowed him a little shoulder barge on the way. Joely turned slowly with an apologetic cringe on her face.

'Don't worry,' I said. 'Are you all right?'

She moulded into an embrace, unfortunately disturbed immediately by light from the opening front door. I thought friendly Alison looked a bit stern.

'Come back to my place,' I whispered to Joely's ear.

'No, no, come in with me. Alison's lovely, I promise.'

'She doesn't know me.'

'Please.'

I gave in and soon we were in the kitchen with Alison, who was in her pyjamas. She was a well-built girl, not fat, haughty-looking but was indeed friendly after all.

'Don't mind Oliver,' Alison told me. 'He's harmless.'

'He's a nuisance,' said a pacing Joely.

I listened to Alison stand up for poor, misunderstood Oliver. It turned out the girls had grown up with him and Joely had dated him on and off for a number of years. What I wanted to know was when the last off had happened. Joely ran through examples of Oliver's strange behaviour, saying he was turning into his alcoholic parents, then she raised her hands.

'Enough. It's been two months now and he still won't accept it. I'll smack him next time.'

'Well, I'll get back to bed,' said Alison. 'Nice to meet you, Alex.'

'And you, Alison.'

'Eight o'clock,' Alison said, kissing Joely goodnight. 'We'll let Oliver follow us round the Bluewater.'

Joely watched her friend go before leaning into me, letting me stroke her hair.

I relaxed in the Victorian Semi's spacious living-room while Joely made tea. My shoes were off and I was sinking into an antique brown leather sofa. It was clear that Alison shared the house with other people. There was a college project spread out on a table, abandoned ironing, a guitar, a full ashtray. It was dimly lit with dark red wallpaper adding to the gloom. I was thinking about fleas in that student gaffe when Joely returned, smiling again and forgetting the visit of Oliver. The tray she placed down had biscuits on it.

'Not Bath Oliver's, I hope.'

She looked blankly at me. 'No, Digestives.' Then she made a derr sound and said, 'I know what Bath Olivers are.'

She set a CD playing softly then joined me, half sitting on my legs but I didn't complain. I watched her adjust her belt and we both smiled because of my liking for the area inside the hip. I forced myself not to think about it, settling for having her close.

'Where are Alison's housemates?' I asked.

'They're under strict instructions not to show themselves.'

I felt extremely relaxed, aware of the lingering aroma of scented candles or Draw. I listened to *The Stereophonics* album. We had our tea, then changed positions to be more reclined together. She struggled with the belt again, amused that I looked away rather than tell her to just take the damn things off.

'Thank you for taking me out,' she said.

'My pleasure. Hey, if you're up early, maybe I should be going.'

'Yeah, but not yet.' She got up. 'Loo, excuse me.'

When she returned she had lost the leather pants and was in just an outsize Arsenal top with round collar in the 1970's style. I ran a hand down my face, finding the sight both incredibly horny and misguidedly horrible.

'Are you seriously an Arsenal fan? Because that's so sad.'

'Of course I am. I always sleep in this.'

'Always?'

She turned to show me *WALCOTT* on her back and I was so dumbfounded that she laughed loudly as she came back to me on the sofa, right down on top of me. I selflessly offered guiding hands to her legs. I waited patiently for her to kiss me with slow touches, her breasts pressing through that thing.

What followed was just cosy chatting, eating up the hours, with a little necking but definitely no full-on snogging. I volunteered to leave a number of times but she couldn't let me go. We heard people moving about and thought we heard somebody outside. Oliver got the blame. We went through other CDs. We heard the milkman.

'How can you go shopping on no sleep?' I asked at one point.

'I could go shopping in my sleep. Don't worry. I'll catch up with my beauty sleep.'

As I cuddled her, happily drifting in and out of clarity and thinking of food again, I puzzled over whether or not the coming day would be better with or without sleep myself.

SIXTEEN

I closed the heavy door of Alison's house as quietly as possible and walked into a fresh morning; the street empty of life. It did cross my mind that Oliver might want to have a go, but then I was in the Ferrari and trying to find my way home. I found it completely inappropriate having the car by then and I was glad to eventually get it around the back of the Takeaway.

I went upstairs to the bedroom, no intention of sleeping, as it was already a sun trap. I changed my clothes into jeans, tee-shirt and trainers, then went for some juice and two bowls of corn flakes. A check on the phone came up with no messages. I moved my bike out to the stairs before going for a pee and splashing some ice-cold water onto my face. I wet back my hair and looked at my appearance in the mirror, feeling withdrawal symptoms from being away from that girl, only wanting it to be right with her, to be free to pursue her without a care in the world. I made a move through the flat, putting on cycling gloves, an old baseball cap and wraparound shades.

I free-wheeled out onto the road. Immediately, I saw Coffee Shop owner Marcus and his wife Kimberley, outside the front of their store chatting with some kind of council official who had a clipboard in hand. Cycling slowly by them, they were all in fairly cheery conversation, so clearly not about to be closed down on hygiene regulations. I decided against spitting on the road and sped up to leave the village quickly, going up the gears, covering the ground to the east. After a couple of miles, I slowed appreciably, submitting to the heat and sweat. There was nobody around, mainly farmland with the occasional big house. No traffic, either, no speeding salesmen, no open convertibles. I started to think of people. I thought of my sister in Manchester. I thought of my ex-girlfriends, some disarmingly sweet and some downright evil. As always, the ones who had treated me with illogical cruelty and selfishness remained uppermost in my mind. Strangely, a vision of Harry Madox behind his bar came along next. That took me onto Carla, which disturbed me, making me look down at my feet moving and the tarmac passing underneath. Sweat stung my eyes. What to do now with Carla? It was all a jumble of emotions that easily gave out to the pleasure and certainty of Joely, and once more I felt like a love-struck teenager. I wanted to be back holding her throughout the night.

I started to get somewhere on the bike, parched parkland with a scattering of redbrick houses, music coming from a gathering of kids, one of those useless female joggers with the sweatband and the water-filled knuckledusters. I cycled on steadily. A Labrador snapped at the unwanted advances of a Boxer. The Labrador was pulled one way by an elderly man while the Boxer went the other with an embarrassed woman.

'He doesn't normally react like that,' the man said to the woman in a retired Major tone. 'But he's not used to getting humped.'

I freewheeled down into a cul-de-sac of small modern houses which were quiet with the residents out working to pay for them. I stopped, wiped my brow above the shades. There was one man there, preparing to hose his lawn. I watched him faff around, wearing Wellingtons but with a checked shirt and proper trousers. I moved towards him and turned the bike in the road so that it was facing outwards. The heart started to pump harder and I fought to think straight through the sensation, letting the bike drop slowly to the pavement between my legs. I wanted to be back holding Joely. When could I be with her again? I focussed myself, looking at the man from behind, judging his height to be similar to my own, looking at the greying hair. A quick scan around, seeing nothing to concern me, no neighbours about to appear. I crossed the pavement towards the man on his drive, feeling a huge rush. Everything closed in around me, all sound excluded. The man sensed me and turned. He had no time to even formulate a question or hardly comprehend the reason for the approach before I acted, before I struck. I gave him a full-handed and incredibly loud slap across the head. The man fell onto his backside in shock, with me already walking away to mount the bicycle and pedal away out of the saddle.

A bad day had by all.

Every mature male face that passed me at Kentmere had to be inspected for bruising. Later, I barneyed with a couple of members for misusing the tennis equipment and, although desirable, the Full Andy Hartson Treatment could not be applied as they were only about fourteen. Then Nervo argued with one woman about litter and her foul-mouthed tirade involved me and Tim. Nervo took it to heart and went home after his shift feeling upset with the world.

At the end of the day there was also a melee in the public car park over a minor bump. Tim joined me on the front lawns to check out the scene.

'Has anyone been run over yet?' he asked.

'No. That's exactly where that woman died. They're fucking clueless.'

'Do you want to go to the pub?'

I rubbed the back of my neck, feeling like I'd had a bit too much sun. I looked around, saw some receptionists going home, Harry Madox arriving, pushing at his damaged mouth after that incident in the bar. Up on the sun terrace I could see Carla collecting glasses. I should really make an effort to talk to her. Macro was up there, talking close to her face while she intermittently played with her hair. Even from that distance I could tell that she was uncomfortable and found it to be strange. She moved away with her glasses and was then warmly accosted by Macro's visiting friend, the cheery Gus, to whom she found a smile and shared some banter, but then her face became stern again as she moved out of view. My tired eyes made me look down again. Maybe I should go home and sleep.

'Hey, there's Gus,' indicated Tim. 'Top man that. Have you met him yet, Alex? He's dead funny, is Gus.'

'Yeah, I've met him.'

'Well, are we off to the pub?'

'Yeah, sure, mate. Where?'

'The Red Lion. I'll have Beth pick me up. Do you want the shower first?'

'No, go on. I'm going up to see Carla.'

I looked up again, Macro and Gus looking out over the grounds. I made my way upstairs but when I got there I found Harry in charge of the bar.

'Carla, Alex, mate? You've just missed her. Go on, be cheeky, check the Ladies.'

I had no joy, so wandered down to hit the shower after Tim. The car park rage was still going on as we were leaving.

'Hit her!' shouted Tim.

Somebody was bibbing their horn. I found Karen Hennessy standing at her car watching the kerfuffle. She waved me over and I stepped onto the rich car park.

'How are you?' I asked.

'I'm good, thank you. What about that murder business?' I just stared at her. 'Poor Mrs Lloyd. Horrible, isn't it?'

'Yes, it is.'

'Just finished?'

'Yes. Been on any picnics recently?'

'No, I can't seem to find the right companions. Would you be free by any chance?'

'Ah.' I watched the silly argument going on. 'Now that would be difficult, at the moment, Karen.'

'That's a shame.'

We looked at each other.

'Got to go, Karen,' I said, moving towards Tim who was not bothering with that woman again. 'Be good.'

'Oh, always, Alex.'

With the Red Lion's beer garden being overcrowded, Tim and I remained inside with our pints, watching the girls with the lads on the pool table as well as some rugby on TV. I listened to my friend waffle on, about work inevitably, and cricket, and then the European hotspots Beth was considering for their holiday.

'Lanzarote,' Tim had got to, 'I heard that's a right dump.'

On cue, the girl herself turned up to collect Tim. She seemed a tad more arsey than usual, I thought, but still amazingly sexy. There was no hello forthcoming. She wore a cream vest that showed a fraction more skin at the side of her chest which I found myself drawn to. While Tim finished his pint I began to feel tetchy with the vibes coming off Beth, wondering what was annoying her now.

'And how are you?' I asked her in a baiting tone.

'Oh, yeah, the charmer, Alex Robateau. Have you seen the state you've left Carla in? She's crazy about you, and you just mess her about something rotten. So much so that she's shagging some old twat at Kentmere.'

I withstood the verbal barrage with an expression of mild chagrin.

'What old twat would that be?'

'I don't know his name. The big boss.'

'Macro?'

'She's a lovely girl and you... you...'

Beth ran out of words and launched herself at me with her trademark left, right slaps. I didn't take offence and fended her off until Tim pulled her clear by the waist. Her body language suggested Tim would be wise to take his hands off her, then she stormed out of the pub, calling, 'Tim! NOW, Tim.'

Tim knew he didn't have to apologise to me. He went after his girlfriend. I bathed in the amused stares of the Red Lion regulars while pensively finishing my beer.

I went home to play ball. I was not upset with Beth, having been slapped by women before, and I didn't feel like one of those poor sods battered by their missus in a packed nightclub. The ball continued to the gloves even though I felt a headache coming on, suddenly realising it was Macro chewing away at my insides, feeling jealousy for that man being near the lovely Carla. What was she playing at? Surely Macro had coerced her in some way. I began to feel the ball on the bones in my hand, pain across the top of my head with every pump of the heart. I found myself shuffling up avenues of thinking and plotting, deciding what to do, struggling to understand why I should do anything at all. I remembered I could take Macro. Say goodbye to Kentmere but I could take Macro. I let the ball through to the curtain. With the "Job" to be done (call it murder, for fuck's sake, I told myself) the idea was to remain normal. What could be more normal than getting sacked and going up on an assault charge for doing the bastard who took advantage of a girl more than half his age?

I threw off the gloves to go for a glass of water. I made a mental note to contact my cricket captain and cry off the last few games. Sport was off the agenda for the time being. Hearing a car pull in, I opened the door, unsure who I wanted to see. Joely would be great. Carla, I wanted it to be Carla. Or Beth come back to apologise and offer up her nubile body to me. It was Joely's black Citroen. I stood still, trying not to incite my throbbing brain to hurt me anymore. I thought of Oliver from Tuesday night. There was an assault to be done there perhaps. Maybe I could do a job lot. Joely appeared with a smile, in casual baggy clothing again and a David Beckham hair band.

'I want you to see my Candy,' she called up.

I cracked up laughing and felt my head split.

SEVENTEEN

I relaxed and let the little Citroen take the strain. I watched Joely's careful driving style. I allowed an age for my eyes to traverse down her profile. There was the delicate feminine forehead with one preened eyebrow, that cute nose, come-to-bed pouty lips. Overall: just lovely. It was another image on my brain that I attempted to store away, maybe for a lonely day some time in my fifties. She caught me looking and broke the pose with a smile.

'Have you been driving long?' I teased.

'No, not long.'

'How's Oliver?'

'Don't know. Don't care.'

We bobbed along country lanes with the two of us quite happy not to make small talk. The bog standard radio was playing something, but it could not be heard above the open windows which were down the perfect degree to leave a pleasant vacuum through my ears.

My thoughts drifted away to Carla and what on earth was going on there. Macro invaded proceedings and accelerated my heart rate, quickly making me steam with anger and annoyance at the man, pondering how to deal with him. I wondered whether Carla was expecting me to deal with him. I sighed and glanced at Joely's concentrating profile again. I should be thinking about her. Macro could wait patiently for me at Kentmere. Joely pulled into an establishment with stables and barns and horrendous smells.

'Here we are,' she said. 'Are we excited?'

'About what?'

'Meeting Candy.' When I paused, she playfully tutted. 'Come on.'

I eased myself from the Citroen. I was wasn't exactly overwhelmed by all things equine, but dutifully stroked the Grey's nose and used words like handsome and personality. I did find Joely's childlike affection for the animal very sweet.

She sensed my boredom and thankfully didn't prolong the visit to Candy's stall, and soon we were walking down the fields quietly talking and flirting, stopping to lounge over a stile before moving on through a small wood. The evening had turned overcast and clammy, and by the time we were on our way back it was light summer rain that bothered neither of us as we kept stopping to kiss and embrace. Back in the car, we went for the full-on snog, hands cupping faces and pulling of hair. Once again I became flushed with fear that it was all going to end early with this girl so I asked for and received permission to touch her, moving a hand inside her top to hold her left breast.

'Joely.'

'Mmm?'

'Do you think Candy would mind?'

'Mind if we have sex in there? No, I don't think so.'

'Shall we, then? Can we, then?'

I kissed all around her neck while she decided. I tried to be patient, until I had to break off to illicit a reply.

'Still thinking. I hadn't planned our first time in there. It's not exactly some romantic hay barn in Tuscany, you know.'

I continued kissing.

'I don't mind if it's dirty,' I said.

'Well I do. There'll be spiders.'

'You big girl's blouse. My place, then?'

Still she hesitated. Was she making the connection between spiders and my flat as well? Now it was dusk and cold and raining on the windshield. She began to drive and I decided against pressing the matter.

On arrival back at my village, I had mild butterflies in my stomach. I chased her up the stairs through a downpour and we bundled through into the flat.

'We should get you out of those wet clothes,' I advised.

Tops went first, allowing me to marvel at the bosom in a cream bra. Joely kissed my muscular chest and shoulders as I backed her towards my bedroom. She seemed happy and normal, although I sensed there was still some barrier she was throwing up, something going on in her mind. Her mild dilemma ceased to concern me as I lowered her to the bed and easily lost her baggy trousers with one hand to find knickers that went high over her beautiful hips. I started to kiss her stomach before she moved some fabric aside to allow me to kiss my favourite area on a girl's body.

Knocking on the door froze us.

'Can I swear?' I asked. 'There's no way I'm seeing who

that is.'

As I said that my mind rushed through all the people it could be. Everyone except the bailiffs would be dreadful right then. We looked at each other, silently saying the usual things like it might be important.

'Whatever it is,' I said, standing, 'doesn't disturb this.'

I came out of the bedroom, seeing nobody through the window in the door, wondering whether that was a good thing. Moving closer I looked out, at one person turned away with a hooded coat on. As I opened the door it was Carla who looked round, then down at my bare chest, then smiled apologetically.

'Hi,' I said, wishing I could bring her in out of the rain.

'Hi. I've not woken you, have I?'

She looked so cute out there with rain making her blink. She did well to decipher my body language and became mortified.

'Oh, God, Alex, I've disturbed you while you're with her. I'm such a twit. Embarrassing...'

I joined her in the rain and cold and stopped her leaving.

'Hey, Carla, what are you doing? We're supposed to be friends, aren't we? I'm sorry, Carla.'

'I'm sorry, Alex. I heard Beth attacked you. You must think I'm a...'

'I don't think you're anything. I'm sorry if I've upset you. Let's meet and talk, tomorrow. Clear up all this crap.'

Carla was crying. She pointed inside. 'She must think I'm a total loon.'

'She doesn't think anything. We'll talk tomorrow,

okay?'

She nodded. I touched her chin.

'Get in out of this, Alex. I'm off.'

'I'm coming for you tomorrow. And stop being upset.'

'I'll try.'

I watched her go before coming in and locking up. I took a towel from a radiator to dry myself off before returning to Joely, who I found with an understandingly sweet expression but lounging there fully clothed. I dropped down next to her.

'Are we disturbed?'

She nodded.

'Do you trust me to get the mood back?'

She shook her head.

I had gone off sex myself. Still, it was reassuring that Joely seemed cool with my domestic complications. Well, she had Oliver after all. She let me snuggle up.

'Alex, this is a girl's room.'

'True. I normally don't hang around long enough for interior design.'

'You know, I want to spend a long time with you.'

'What, you mean like get married?'

'No, dummy. I mean days on end. Can we go somewhere together?'

'Christ, I wanted to take you to Heaven but you didn't want to go.'

'Heaven? We'll see about that. What about a holiday?'

'Italy.'

'Italy.'

I sat up, pausing for effect.

'A romantic hay barn in Tuscany,' I mocked.

She winced.

'Don't take the piss, boy.'

We kissed and she made me settle back down, where I stayed for an hour before she left. I got wet again watching her down to the Citroen and then drive out. A night freight train came through.

I sat with coffee in my springy chair watching rain against the gloom, then I went through and slept a little before dawn.

I set off cycling to Kentmere way too early, thinking about love, friendship and retribution; Joely, Carla and Macro in that order. On arrival, I saw Macro's Jag parked next to Carla's Beetle. While I stopped to ponder that little coincidence I was hailed from the nearest tennis court.

'Hello there!' It was Macro's friend, Gus. His tennis gear carried red and blue stripes down the side, as if he was playing in the 1982 football World Cup. 'Be a sport, old man, and throw us that ball back.'

I located the errant ball and threw it over the mesh fence.

'Thanks, Alex.'

'No problem.'

'Are you all right? You look mad at the world.'

I looked at him, and at the vaguely familiar member further up the court. I started my bike in the direction of the building.

'I'm fine, thank you,' I called back to him.

Nobody bothered me on the way to my office where I

put the kettle on, listening to some member of staff singing *Someone Like You*. I stripped for a cold shower, letting the jet fire against my hot neck as I stood leaning against the tiles. I was unable to shake Macro, coming to a sudden resolution to confront the man and warn him off Carla, I stepped out, intending to quickly towel down and dress damp to go and speak my mind, but I found Carla there, leaning shyly against the doorframe. I covered myself, swept back my hair and then drip-dried as we looked at each other.

'He's a cunt,' I said after a moment.

'It doesn't matter what he is. Let it pass, please, Alex.'

'I just want to make him understand. That you're special to me. That, I don't know, that he... shouldn't.'

I made a move for another towel but she thought I was going for Macro in a semi-naked state and stopped me with spread fingers to my wet chest.

'Do you remember what you said at the playing fields?' she asked, not removing her hands. 'You said we should go with the flow. Friends that don't have to ask. Everything's fine.'

'Was this the Adam and the Ants day?'

'It was.'

'Well, actually, I remember...'

She stopped me with a kiss which I responded to with hands to the face, pleased my towel had stayed up. Our momentum took us along the wall, dropping clipboards and Nervo's spare overalls, furiously kissing, with nowhere else to go but the shower. Carla seemed intense. She unfurled the top of my towel and forced it away to the floor. I was slightly taken aback as I watched her strip, with the door still open and *Someone Like You* sounding nearer. I stepped back into the shower to absolve myself of any blame. Blame, guilt, Joely, Carla, now with knickers as always last to peel off before she joined me and set the water flowing. I could see she was nervously gasping, maybe at the water, her hair changing tone and damping down on her face to make her look even more appealingly vulnerable. She kissed me back against the cold tiles and pressed all her body up against mine.

A loud whistle, one that would have needed the fingers in the mouth, shocked us from the corridor. Carla leant out from the shower and flashed her nakedness to a grinning Tim. Any attempt at covering herself would have had her falling on the floor so she didn't bother.

'Too High approaching,' Tim warned, without averting his gaze.

We towelled down frantically, both of us giggling. Carla, laughing, pushed Tim out to the corridor before we threw on some clothes and made ourselves look decent. I saw Tuohy mince by without looking in, then *Someone Like You* died an unnatural death.

The day had turned out very humid with a hazy sun. Out on the grounds, I wiped sweat from my eyes as I thought again about being with Carla in the office.

'Alex,' called an approaching Karen Hennessy. 'Do you do foreigners?'

'Foreigners? Yes, foreigners, English girls, the occasional Welsh bird.'

'No, you know, moonlighting jobs. I want you and your lads to sort out my garden. I'll pay you handsomely, handsome.'

I had decided not to attack my boss. I had escaped with being caught in a compromising position. I decided I should maintain appearances and snatch the money out of her hand.

'We'll do that for you, Karen.'

'Oh, good.'

EIGHTEEN

One afternoon while out in the grounds, I again found myself contemplating all the distractions to the matter at hand: loving Joely, coveting Carla, having to work, being the local gigolo, when there approached a vision across the grass, as stunning as it was unexpected, with the disc of the sun providing a background halo. It was Chloe, my Manchester Ex, looking fine in a dark business suit, impeccably groomed and even carrying a shiny briefcase.

'Fuck me,' I said. 'Have you become a solicitor?'

'No, stupid,' she said in a friendly tone. 'I'm still with the travel agents. And before you ask, your sister told me about this place. Don't have a go at her, I forced it out of her.'

I realised I was shirtless and glistening, my dungarees rolled a fraction too low. Politely but coldly, I asked, 'What brings you down here?'

'I'm on a two-day conference in Milton Keynes.'

'How grim is that?'

'I know. This is day one.'

'What's day two, torturing small animals?'

She smiled, then looked around the grounds.

'How much are the fees, anyway?' I stared her out. 'Is there somewhere we can talk, Alex?'

'We're in the middle of a field. It can't get any more private.'

She went into the briefcase, as if she was about to serve me papers, but just pulled out a mint.

'I was wondering, Alex, if you'd like to meet up tomorrow.' She paused. 'That would be day two.' My dumbfounded silence seemed to encourage her. 'We could, you know, have a drink for old times sake. I've got a hotel room.'

'Where's whatsisface on this little junket?'

'If by that you mean Jason, he's working hard at his new business.'

'I'm sure he's doing very well.'

'He is, as a matter of fact.'

I took a swig of water, then gestured for her to continue.

'I just thought it would be nice, while I was down here. Or you could come at lunchtime, if you want, and we could go up to my room.'

Now there certainly was a distraction from the matter at hand. I explored the cut of her suit and watched her lips sucking the mint. I began to wander about on the spot, now with too much information to think about: my Chloe Green in a hotel room, Joely, Carla, working, murder contract, my gigolo career. It was astonishing that she was there, never mind making those kind of suggestions.

'Do you want a reply straight away?' I asked before I'd even cleared my head of the woman's illogical behaviour.

'No rush. But before day two would be helpful. Are you going to show me around while I'm here?'

I stared at her. 'What the hell – come on.'

I threw on my top and we headed in. Mathew Molina

was one of the ten or so people on the courts to watch us pass. 'Tennis courts,' I said. 'Man up a ladder, my assistant, Tim.'

I took her in through reception and named the department. The tour proceeded through the indoor courts, the gym and the wet rooms, finishing in the bar, with Carla not on duty and only sour-faced Rachel Calderbank to give us a dirty look. 'Rachel behind the bar. You two would get on like a house on fire.'

Day two. While showering, I tried to visualise Joely's body, but all I got was the hair in bunches and the provocative pout. I just wanted her with me. Towelling down, I found myself wondering how boring a travel agents' conference could be. My coffee was waiting for me and out on the stairwell I think it was Joss Stone playing early on from Miss Brocklebank's. It was a glorious day. The Job, the Contract, the Murder, was out there across the fields, blended with the beautiful summer colours of yellow and green and tan brown. I kept the Job, the Contract, the Murder light and distant because there was something else to do that day. I had woken out of my special Chloe dream, and out there on the stairwell with a warm breeze washing my face I thought again of the happiness and thrill that always gave me.

I decided to go off and cycle my usual route, making sure to spit at the Coffee Shop on returning. After an early lunch, I showered again and paid full attention to my grooming. Dressed in my best jeans and a new shirt, and even with my Rockports polished, I drove off into sunny

Surrey.

It didn't take me long to come to my imposing destination, in a few acres of prime land with a red Tudor brick wall stretching from view both ways. I was buzzed in and drove slowly up to the big house surrounded by large willow trees and with a picturesque brook that went trilling along.

Nichola Duckinfield came out to greet me with a hug. She looked tanned and happy; well, she did have me there after all. She was dressed in flimsy cream blouse and short pale skirt.

'Great house,' I said.

She shrugged as she led me in.

'Come through, Alex.'

'Thank you for the invite.'

'Glad you could make it. I know how highly prized your time is.'

'Yes, there was somewhere else I was supposed to be.'

'Have you eaten?'

'Yes, thanks. So, I trust the hubby's busy working.'

'He's at his office with his lawyers.'

'Lawyers? Sounds heavy.'

She took me to the kitchen with its marble worktops and a gargantuan American fridge. The French windows were open to a virtual woodland of a garden. Long sheds for a serious horticultural hobby stood one side of the brook with a stable block on the other. I sat on a stool, nodded when offered orange juice and listened to Joss Stone again on the radio.

'Where's your son?' I asked.

'Out adventuring with his friends.'

'No Au Pairs, cleaners in?'

'No, why?'

'All alone, then?'

We made small talk about the house and about that night's Italian lesson, of all things. Eating home-made cookies, she showed me the part of the garden within sight of the house, but I declined to see the horses. Amid the privacy of the gardening sheds I took the opportunity to tenderly touch her belly under the hem of the flimsy top. The flash in her eyes told me she was still excited by our friendship. She gently took hold of my face to give me a kiss.

'Not working today?' she asked.

'I am, actually, right now. But I'm being very hard to pin down for some reason.'

'Don't you have a pager?'

'No.'

'Well, like I say, I'm glad you could make it. I'll try to make the afternoon interesting, before I go off and do my Italian class.'

'Nichola, did you bring me here to talk about learning Italian?'

'No, no,' she flustered, and with a smile led me up the garden path back towards the house.

Squealing bicycle tyres and children's shouts stopped us and bounced her away from me. A group of boys appeared through the willow trees.

'My son and his gang.'

'Not great adventurers it seems.'

She strode off to deal with them, calling back, 'Be a landscape gardener.'

'I beg your pardon?'

'If any of the lads speak to you. Be a landscape gardener.'

'Understood.'

I lingered around in the garden watching Nichola doing first aid on two of the boys who had apparently fallen off something.

'Tree surgeon,' I said to the first boy who approached me without waiting to see if he was interested or not.

Nichola came across and put a motherly arm around the boy.

'Well, Mr Smith?'

'I've examined the damaged tree, Mrs Duckinfield.'

'You've examined the tree?'

She turned to her son.

'Mum, can we just hang out here because of what happened to Eddie and Cheese?'

What could she do but nod?

'Mrs Duckinfield,' I interjected. 'If I could just show you the trouble.'

'Yes, of course, Mr Smith.'

She allowed me to steal her away towards the greenhouses, her walking with arms firmly crossed.

'Has your son got a friend called Cheese?'

'Yes, silly nickname, isn't it.'

I was still in the mood, kissing her neck once we were amongst the steel and plant-entangled glass, Nichola straining to monitor the whereabouts of all the boys.

'My God, Alex, what are we doing?'

I backed her into one of the greenhouses.

'We can't,' she said, even as she responded with her own crazed kissing.

Young voices could be heard and Nichola wanted me in a panic, guilt-stricken and furtively glancing between sunflowers.

'We can't, Alex.'

I lifted her easily and plopped her down on a mucky shelf.

'Keep watch,' I told her, slipping my hands up her bare thighs, seeking to remove her panties but there were none to remove. I forced the skirt up around her waist with a little help from her dainty little hop.

'I'm on soil,' she said, not complaining but nervous, still watching out as the voices became more boisterous. I knelt amid flowerpots and pulled her forward to a better position.

'Oh, Alex, yes.' Her hands went to my head as I took my mouth down. 'Be quick,' she gasped, then, 'No, don't be quick. Oh my God. Bloody hell, someone's coming, no, they've run off again.' Then her words became quite incoherent.

'The day's gone,' complained Nervo from the back of my Audi as we sped towards Walton-On-Thames. 'Why couldn't we start this morning?'

Tim turned up the music to drown him out.

We were on our way to do Karen Hennessy's garden. The day was decidedly cool, making me think that maybe that was it for summer. I pulled into Karen's road, finding it lined with cars. I thought it just like her to have girlfriends round for cocktails while we toiled in the garden.

As we started to unload the boot I could hear laughter and chatter. Drifting along the drive I saw a white canopy covering a social gathering. Then Karen came out to us, all happy and dressed up.

'Alex, hi. Gentlemen. I'll own up straight away. I've gotten you here under false pretences. We're having drinks and a barbecue. More the merrier, I thought.' I looked at both my friends while Karen went on with herself. Nervo was puzzled and thinking how to get away. Tim's expression hinted that he was thinking champagne. 'Seemed a shame to cancel you. I'll pay you, of course.'

'Excellent,' said Tim.

Karen looked at him with his crew cut, leaning back in his old boots.

'There are clothes you can all change into, Alex.'

Attending a barbecue was just as normal as gardening to me.

'Fine, Karen. Thank you. Give us a minute to put the gear away.'

She went back to her guests. Tim was smiling away, while Nervo clearly wanted to go. I knew better than to try to talk him into staying. I offered up my car keys.

'Do you want to take the car? We'll find our own way back.'

Tim and I watched my Audi leave, before I nudged him and we removed our boots. The French Nanny, Anne-

Marie, led us into the house. I wondered if she remembered me from my last visit. She now had a shorter, trendier haircut.

'In here, please,' she said.

She left us in a bedroom where a selection of men's clothes was laid out on the bed. Tim wandered around the room, finally stopping to tap on the big mirror against one wall.

'What are you doing?' I asked.

'I'm imagining all the other guests standing the other side of this. What's the game here, man?'

'Nothing. Free booze and food. Just enjoy yourself. This woman has good-looking girls working for her. They should be here.'

'Who's the French bird?'

'Au Pair or something. Come on, get your Gimp suit on.'

We dressed in black trousers and pale summer shirts and hesitantly joined the party which consisted of about forty people. Tim was lagging behind me.

'What's wrong now?' I asked.

'These shoes are two sizes too big.'

I stopped a passing waiter with a tray of champagne. As Tim took his glass he said, 'Cheers, Martin.'

'What the fuck are you doing here?' whispered waiter Martin.

'I was invited.'

Tim shuffled me towards a gaggle of beauties, where Karen paused in passing to ask Tim which one he would like to be introduced to. He pretended to take offence.

'I'm with someone, thank you very much, but the one in the flowery dress looks very nice.'

'That's Laura.'

'Who are these people?' I asked her.

'Some are friends, some are business contacts. Be patient, guys, the square people won't stay all day. Where's Nerdo got to?'

'It's not his scene, Karen. He's a very shy man.'

'Oh, dear. I thought I had a chance there.'

She mimed "later" as she was stolen away. I sat on a low wall, watching Tim sidle off towards the girls. I sipped my wine, listening to a vociferous group of men discuss the laws on speed humps.

'How are they allowed?' enquired one man with passion. 'They block the highway. They stop me doing thirty miles an hour.'

'And the damage they cause,' said another. 'There's one near my home that scrapes exhausts all day long. I tell you what, all rounds should be clear, except around schools, and they should just give the birch to the boy racers.'

'And parking on grass verges has increased. That really upsets me.'

I noted two late-comers. Nichola Duckinfield and Tina Molina arrived at the same time, but not together judging by the way they said hello to each other. They were dressed similar in white cotton tops and blue jeans, but Tina had the look of a Spanish flamenco dancer with her blouse pulled down off her shoulders. She noticed me and waved with a smile before people engulfed her, and Nichola air-kissed a few acquaintances before making her way across to me. I wanted to shout “potting shed!” but restrained myself.

‘Didn’t expect to see you here,’ she said, smiling.

I returned the smile from my seated position. The memory of our last meeting gave me a thrill. She must have been thinking the same thing.

‘I was Shanghaied. Are you friends with Karen?’

‘Not really. But you don’t turn down invitations from Karen Hennessy.’

‘On your own?’

‘Yes.’

Surprised at how pleased I was to see her, I clasped my hands together gently round the back of her thighs. There was the briefest of self-conscious glances round before she caressed my head. Then the efficient Martin was there with a drink which she accepted before taking her place beside me on the wall.

Nichola let me in on the gossip of our fellow guests. I laughed with her, and sat back and watched as she playfully bitched, noting that she was growing her hair and had caught the sun. When she got round to the girls with Tim I looked across to see my friend moving off to the bottom of the garden with Laura, no doubt to have a private smoke.

I spent most of the afternoon with Nichola, eating and drinking. We commandeered a sun lounger and sat chatting away with Karen’s stereo playing from the house. Inevitably, one of the subjects she drew out of me was Joely and I easily obliged with all the details, pleased to have someone as genuine as Nichola to open up to. She felt like an old friend.

When Tim and Laura eventually emerged from the shrubbery, most of the guests had drifted home and the caterers were packing up. Nichola sat up from my chest, disturbing my reverie.

'Do you think I've put in enough time?' she asked.

'What, with me?'

'No, at Karen's party.'

'So you're going?'

'I have to.'

We slowly stood and hugged. Tim had something important to tell us.

'Hey, there's a beautiful stream down there. You should check it out. It's lovely down there.'

Nichola smiled at the young man before concentrating her attentions on me, touching my face in a blatant gesture of closure, which I accepted.

'Enjoy this Joely girl,' she said. 'Be happy, Alex.'

We kissed and then I let her go home.

NINETEEN

That was one comfortable lounger out there on Karen Hennessy's patio. Before I knew it, I was virtually alone in the early evening shade, thinking maybe I should have gone, but I'd had too much to drink to drive home, and besides, I didn't have a car, so I relaxed back again.

A still happy Tim came back out to me.

'Hey, Alex, we're going in the Jacuzzi.'

'Fuck off, Tim.'

'Come on, I know you want to.'

'Who's going in the Jacuzzi?'

'Not sure yet. The French bird's getting changed. Come on, I know where there are trunks.'

'I need more booze if I'm going in a Jacuzzi.'

'Champagne coming right up.'

I had a rueful smile to myself. What the hell, I thought. Tim went off on his mission. I stood and wandered through the living area, looking down again into Karen's bizarre glass well in the wooden floor and then reacquainting myself with her daughter's rear in the arty photo.

Tim was already stripped to baggy blue shorts when he reappeared with the alcohol, causing me to laugh at him.

'Go back in that same room,' he advised me. 'Then the wicked sauna-Jacuzzi room is at the end of the hall.'

I quaffed my champagne, then went through, again

considering just going home. In the bedroom, I encountered Anne-Marie hurrying to conceal her naked top half with her bathing costume.

'I'm sorry,' I apologised.

'You want next door.'

'Right, then.'

I changed into black shorts before tip-toeing down the hall into the Jacuzzi room, where Tim boisterously welcomed me from the bubbling water with his arm around Laura, as they drank from crystal flutes. A coy Anne-Marie was the only other person there. Who's minding the kid, I thought. Does she think it's her lucky night? I lowered myself into the wonderful frothing water and accepted yet another drink from Tim's seemingly unlimited supply, toasting them all, including the obviously sober Anne-Marie.

'Are you not drinking?' I asked her.

'I do not drink.'

I relaxed with my arms outstretched. Hearing rain on a glass roof, I looked up to see motley shadows of rocking branches. The music being pumped through had me thinking of the time in the Club wet room with Carla, with her soaked hair and flushed pretty face. The door opened, admitting Karen in a black bikini. Her pale, slender figure carefully slid down between Anne-Marie and myself.

'That's good,' said Karen with a sigh. 'Timothy, where's my drink?' Once suitably supplied, she clinked glasses with me. 'There you go. I told you the square people wouldn't stay long.'

I looked properly at Laura for the first time, as the

buxom blonde lifted out of the water in a skimpy bikini top to let Tim whisper to her, then she laughed. I said to Tim, 'You've found your spiritual home.'

'Too right I have, mate.'

I then looked to the strangely content Anne-Marie, finding her plainness sexy in its own way, French women being more earthy anyway, then Karen touched my arm.

'I never thought I'd get you here again,' she said. 'You've been avoiding me.'

'You reckon?'

'But I'll forgive you.'

I watched her take a seductively slow sip of champagne and started to ponder the best way to back her off a little, but being as I was sitting in her Jacuzzi it probably wasn't the best time. I shifted position, inadvertently touching the fingers of her left hand which she linked with mine. Then she took Anne-Marie's hand.

'Everyone,' said Karen. 'Alex is starting a séance. Hold hands.'

Laura laughed and said, 'Is anybody there?'

There came a bang as Tina Molina entered the room in a multi-coloured one-piece costume.

'Room for a small one?' she asked, sliding in beside me. I hid my surprise, thinking she had already left. We had met once during the afternoon, squeezing past each other on the stairs as I headed to the toilet. With a hand slowly traversing my forearm she had jokingly threatened to scratch Nichola's eyes out if she monopolised any more of my time. I had made promises to talk to her. In the Jacuzzi her make-up seemed out of place, with the curly hair up on top of her head. I smiled when she turned her eyes onto me.

'Champagne?' Tim offered Tina.

'Charlie?'

'No, it's Tim.' He knew exactly what she meant.

'Charlie. Coke. Karen, I'm relying on you. And what's this bleeding thing you've put me in?' She roughly fiddled with the elasticated material across her chest, then drank deeply and laughed. 'It'll be off soon, anyway.' She touched my shoulder. 'Only joking.'

Laura suddenly piped up with, 'This is just like Big Brother.'

Tim laughed and agreed. Everyone was happy to sit back and listen to her recount with passion famous incidents from previous years in the reality household. After a while, Tina floated to me to enquire about what had happened to my time that afternoon. We chatted quietly underneath Laura's talking, and in a round the houses way and without naming Joely I delivered the message that while it had been great fun flirting there would be nothing happening between myself and Tina. She briefly playacted a sulk on my shoulder, then she gave me a "we'll see" expression before turning her attentions to Laura's waffling.

'Not even a one-off snog?' Tina came back to me with.

I smiled at Tina, her cheeky demeanour reminded me of the silly side of life. I wondered what it would have been like to meet her a few years ago before she went up in the world. I obliged with a brief snog. I thought of Joely, my imagination making her praise me and say "good boy, that's two down, anyway".

Under the camouflage of Tina rabbitting on to Laura, I turned to Karen, seeing her perspiring and I recalled our steamy session in my flat. Her face carried an expression of resignation; nevertheless she whispered, 'I'm getting jealous.'

'I was just telling Tina I'm spoken for.'

'Does that apply to me?' When I nodded she gave my shoulder muscle a nostalgic squeeze. 'Oh, well.'

'I've not offended you, have I?'

'God, no.' She affectionately brushed my face. 'Oh, and I won't be needing a farewell kiss, by the way.'

Karen leant over to Anne-Marie where the French girl was more than happy to share a lingering kiss.

Tim was laughing. 'Who's the French bird?'

I got naked in the bedroom, looking around with my sodden shorts in my hand, finally deciding to just dump them in a sink. There was a small towel handy for a quick rub-down, then I dressed damp in my work clothes and headed out, unconcerned about pneumonia as I stepped into a cold rainstorm, thinking more of leaving my "brother" Tim behind.

My usual taxi firm had sent my usual driver to annoy neighbours with three loud blasts of the horn.

'Had to be you,' said the sardonic driver.

I laughed. As the driver u-turned his Toyota, the headlights slashed along the windswept country lane.

'That's summer done for, then,' said the driver.

'True.'

I realised the light had illuminated a silver Renault Megane with the spare wheel in place. I looked over my shoulder but the rear view was impossible with the storm and sparse street lighting.

'Forget something?' asked the driver.

If the taxi had continued on I might have let the situation pass, despite being thrown into complete turmoil by it. It was a fact that the Megane from my village was there at Karen's that night. Maybe it was another Megane? A puncture was a puncture.

'Go back,' I said.

As the taxi reversed I considered all the options I could think of. If this had something to do with the Job, did I really need to see who was in the Megane? It did if it turned out to be CID. Was I being followed? Was it one person or two? There was no more time to think as the taxi stopped and the driver's round face was between the seats keen to see what I was up to.

I went out into the gale, noting with chagrin that the elements were pushing me towards the Megane. The car started its engine. Oh, you fucking idiot, I thought, you've put yourself out here to be run over. I kept approaching, the back of my head taking the full shower, finally seeing two figures and, as the passenger raised a hand, the driver cut the engine and stepped out. He was big and black and I was up to him.

'Back the fuck away,' said the black man.

I saw the futility of conversation and also ruled out the Full Andy Hartson Treatment as the man wore a thick leather coat. Instead I put in a vicious kick to the groin and the man dropped like a tranquilised rhino. The passenger came out slowly into the rain, with his hands up and all calming. I turned and recognised with a start Mathew Molina.

'Molina?'

'What are you doing, Alex?'

'I could ask you the same thing.'

I checked that the black man was still down, then put a hand up to stop Molina approaching.

'I'm here to pick my wife up,' said Molina calmly. 'Is that all right with you?'

For a second I felt as if I had made a classic fool of myself. Then I remembered the Megane outside the Red Lion. The rain changed direction and we were left standing there on a quiet street staring at each other. The black man was still winded, good. The taxi driver was out of his vehicle looking on.

'You've been expecting her to come out of my flat.'

'I think you're very much mistaken, Alex.'

I kicked the Megane's spare wheel. 'I don't think so.'

Molina smiled, hesitated, then as good as admitted defeat. 'It's not what you think.'

'I don't know what I think.'

'Let's talk. Get into the car.'

I judged the black man's agony about to subside, shook my head at Molina.

'You want to talk to me, we'll talk in the taxi.'

'Fine.'

I handed the driver a twenty to pre-empt any objections and asked to be driven around. Molina was less than happy to have a third party listening in, but he sat in the back of the taxi gathering his thoughts under my malevolent stare.

'Go on, then,' I prompted. 'What do you want?'

'A proposition for you, Alex. About Tina.'

The driver shuffled to hear better.

Molina smoothed away rainwater from his trouser leg, cleared his throat. 'I know her, Alex. I know she's bored, and I would prefer some...control, some limiting effect, no that's wrong, well, some limiting on the damage to me with her future infidelity.'

The driver scratched his head.

'What are you saying?' I asked.

'My Goodtime Girl, you see. She made a suggestion recently. It involved two guys we know, friends of mine, a Mr Bow... well, you don't need to know their names. Either of them was to be... invited to participate in a... threesome at the Molina residence. Now, while these gentlemen are both handsome buggers...' He laughed loudly. 'I'd much prefer to invite someone like you along, Alex.'

We drove for another minute. I'd heard it all now, I thought. I watched the quiet silhouette across the cab.

'Do you want my reply straight away?'

'No, no, take as much time as you want.'

The driver assumed it was the right time to head back into Walton-On-Thames. Molina was dropped at the end of Karen's road.

'Just go,' I told the driver.

TWENTY

I heard the storm a few times during the night, as well as a cat fight and a freight train going through. The street had been checked before retiring, seeing rain lashing a number of cars, but none of them a silver Megane. I went to sleep the first time thinking everything through, round and round in my head, aware of dreaming, the last one staying with me of an argument in a Jacuzzi between a black Big Brother contestant and a girl called Laura.

I sat up suddenly feeling dreadful, sweating, my ankles painfully crossed and needing to be gingerly separated. There was the sound of a hydraulic lift off the back of a truck and then Chinese voices. I started to think of that old man slapped to the ground out on my dry-run. Why was I having pangs of guilt about that? I rubbed my face vigorously.

Two days earlier, I had responded to an advert in a local free newspaper for a 10-speed racer going for twenty odd quid. I had my regular taxi driver take me to the seller's address, where I found the bike in perfect condition, didn't haggle and rode it home.

I packed a rucksack with bottled water and energy biscuits and rode the racer out of the village the morning after the storm. Over breakfast, the incident with Molina had been somewhere in my weary subconscious, then as I turned the gear I was thinking of the advice gathered on my day trip to see Jimmy Sheridan in Salford; that when I was going to look at this man Mathers, to reconnoitre his home and his workplace, to take it for granted that somewhere along the line my image would be recorded. Whether on a traffic monitoring camera, or a neighbour's home security CCTV, somewhere I would be placed near the crime.

'I live close anyway,' I'd tried to mitigate to Keith Jacques, in his dentist waiting room.

'Don't play silly buggers,' he had said close to my face, briefly no longer that newly qualified hygienist. 'No need for fucking brinksmanship.'

After the barney outside Jimmy's flat we had arrived at the local McDonald's. Three teenage girls crossed our path, one calling, 'All right, Jimmy.' I was taken aback – they were absolutely stunning. All in short skirts with jewellery; two in knee-length boots. They had beautiful faces but were clearly as rough as fuck. Was that a shame?

'Ladies,' he had acknowledged with a smile, completely unperturbed by the recent fight.

Keith Jacques was clear that I was not to go in my own car and to cover my features somehow. I had momentarily considered using Tim's scooter before rejecting it with memories of a crash on Corfu when I was a teenager. So I cycled towards Candlesby with a back-to-front baseball cap and wraparound shades, along deserted winding lanes that bisected corn fields and yellow rapeseed fields. It was early with the hot day not yet rid of the storm residue, the earthy smell filling my nostrils. I drifted back briefly onto the shenanigans of Mathew Molina before a small private petrol station brought Keith's words rushing back. I imagined myself happily cycling along with a date and the time in the corner of the screen, and so made sure to be looking away.

Candlesby began with a grey church, uneven gravestones and a mossy boundary wall. With no cars in sight, I pictured myself back in 1898 on a Penny Farthing, going to have tea with a girl who looked like Jenny Agutter from *The Railway Children*. It was a leafy main road, black and white mock Tudor homes hidden away. Still no cars, except for a magnificent silver Audi TT Quattro, and no people. I rode to the far end where there were two side streets before the main road forked either side of a disused Post Office. The first pedestrians were here but they paid me no notice; then I took the right fork, fully intending to check out the other routes later but unable to resist my first look at The Mount. I found more modern huge houses and, typically for a rich area, the road was pot-holed and needing to be slalomed. While sheltered by hedges, I played my ace, fixing in place one of those cyclists' smog masks, completely inappropriate for the countryside but doing the trick nicely. I counted up the houses on the left, assuming that my image was now being recorded and aiming my head with impunity at the security gates. I deliberately went past No. 9, Squirrel's Chase, the Mathers' residence. Outside a quiet No. 11 I dismounted and squatted to pretend to be playing with the gears. The drive of No. 13 dropped away with a public footpath alongside. The house was surrounded by wooded fence rails like in cowboy films with two marble horse heads as gateposts denoting the owner's passion for riding. The houses on the other side were of equal size and just as security conscious, and were mostly deserted apart from an elderly man in his garage.

I returned my attention to No. 9, with a detached double garage the size of my flat. Part of the rear gardens were visible dipping away into dark green foliage. The heavy electric gates impacted on me most: problem, but what were my alternatives? Above the chemist in busy Twickenham? Where he parked his car in busy Twickenham? Another public area at the man's golf club? This was the place, I decided. Where did that public footpath go? My observation returned again to those gates, a barrier to a knock on the door.

The elderly man was out of his garage with a lawnmower. I took off down the public footpath without encountering any pensioners to take offence. It came out of the trees at a river and then took me past a small factory producing cane furniture. Further on ran a dual-carriageway but I came the other way and appeared out of one of those side streets at the disused Post Office. Straight across into the other one which turned into a dead end, I went on the second leg of my reconnaissance. On the congested roads I played the part of annoying cyclist commuter, making use of the cycle lanes (especially the ones three-foot in length) and getting into Twickenham in good time. It was getting warm now, road works causing chaos on the route in from the south. I found the place I was looking for and leant against a wall while looking up to the office above the chemist, its entrance a single doorway with a video entry system.

I pulled down the smog mask, watching the well-heeled folk of Twickenham go by. I swigged water, fascinated by the passers-by, not seeing too much ostentation. I liked Twickenham for some reason. The passing girls who came with designer gear still had mobile phones attached to their heads. There was no blue Saab in the immediate vicinity. After a few minutes I moved on along the road behind the chemist. An expensive looking baby shop had a couple of parking spaces, one of which contained a blue Saab. Possibly Mathers had an agreement to park there. I stopped further up the street to look back. There were shops on both sides and the road seemed to be used by motorists cutting through. I found it decidedly congested.

I vetoed a visit to Mathers' golf club; the Mount in Candlesby being the location, location, location, and besides I was knackered. I considered myself fit but that had been a trip of Tour De France scale.

There was music as I freewheeled down the side of the Takeaway, coming from Joely's Citroen with the girl herself sitting with doors and sunroof open and her feet up on the dash, legs bare and partially covered by denim skirt. The tune was *Flying Without Wings* by Westlife. She smiled but declined to break off listening. I heaved my pumped up thighs from the bike and waddled back and forth, liking the tune despite my usual aversion to Irish boy bands. I lost the shades, then in an afterthought pulled the mask from around my neck, leaving it on the handlebars as I put the racer back under the stairs.

'That's such a beautiful song,' she said as she unfolded her frame to join me in a hug. 'I've loved it from day one, you know, unlike songs that grow on you or songs you like and then start to hate. Did you have a good ride?'

'I didn't expect you.'

'We need to talk.'

'We need to talk?'

'Yeah, and thanks for asking, I've been waiting here half an hour.' She followed me up the stairs. 'I couldn't even find Mr Yu for a nibble.'

I laughed. 'You couldn't even find Mr Yu for a nibble.'

I managed to peel off my shirt while Joely headed for the fridge.

'Can this talk wait until I've showered?'

'Of course.'

As I enjoyed the shower, I had forgotten that Joely was actually in the flat, until she knocked on the bathroom door. Jesus, not only was she there but she's thinking very bad things, and the thought of anything taking place in the bathroom filled my mind with Carla in my office and flushed me with guilt.

'Alex, it's the telephone.'

'Right.'

I towelled off and put on some shorts, deciding against asking her who it was. Whoever it was, Joely obviously found them engaging enough until I took the phone from her with a mock snatch, watching her go out to the stairwell where she seemed to have built a love nest out of pillows.

It was Tim inviting me Pitch and Putting with the gang, although I didn't consider myself to be part of a gang any more. Tim thought it a done deal anyway now with Joely keen to play.

'Is Beth going?' I asked.

'Yeah, so what?'

'Well, I don't think it would be a good idea.'

'Screw Beth. Get this Joely tart out, boy.'

'All right, we'll see.'

I combed my hair and put on a tee-shirt. Before joining Joely I got a coke, first looking to see that she already had a drink. I sank down fatigued, accepting her legs over me.

'Are we going playing golf?' she asked.

'If you want to. Have you played before?'

'That would be a no, but you can teach me. Show me the correct way to do it.' I laughed. 'What are you laughing at?'

'I had a vision of you waggling a club between these beautiful legs.'

'These beautiful not so tanned legs of mine. That's what we have to talk about. I want to take you away on holiday, somewhere hot.'

'You want to take me? You mean pay for me?'

'If you haven't got a problem with that.'

'How can you pay on McDonald's wages?'

'Don't talk about money. I've got big holiday plans for you, Mr Rubber Toe.'

'Could you be more specific?'

'You know, on the beach at midnight, wink, wink.'

I started to kiss her thighs. 'I've got plans for you right

here.'

'Oi, bad boy. Are we going, or what?'

'Well, tell me where.'

'No, I'll surprise you.'

'Well, tell me when.'

'Tomorrow, next week, whenever.'

I looked out across the countryside. This had possibilities as well as problems. Up until then I had been working off a loose schedule. Now plans might have to be timed. I would still need some good fortune, but what could be better than flying away with Joely the day after the Job. I pushed her a little bit more. 'I'll need to know the day of the flight because of work.'

'We won't be flying to Brighton, stupid.'

'Wey-hey!' I nuzzled her thighs, causing her to giggle.

I easily talked Joely out of hitting fake yellow golf balls in the general direction of sun-ravaged and motley greens, and besides, we were incredibly comfortable with a gorgeous westerly breeze and, courtesy of Tim's recipe, a couple of strawberry/Oreo cookie smoothies. We had shared more positions than dreaming sleepers, talking on a variety of subjects, or not talked at all, I had done my toe-pressing job on her, and finally she was on top of me, two fingers playing with my lips.

'What are you thinking?' I asked.

She contemplated for a moment. 'I'm thinking... God, how strong and warm you feel.'

'Go on.'

'No.'

'Go on, please.'

'Turning me on. Feeling like we're already making love. Being dominated...' She turned away with a giggle and I got a face-full of hair. She came back smiling. '...penetrated.'

'Really?'

Her perfume intoxicated me once more, she moulded onto me, she was so fresh. We kissed without knowing we were kissing, lower legs entwined. I stretched just enough to be able to caress impossibly silken skin below the risen denim skirt, feeling one thigh move up my hip. She briefly withdrew from a kiss, so we focussed on each other, I traversing her feline nose to delicate eyebrows and pure skin of her forehead; she going the other way by my mouth and stubble, my firm neck and muscular shoulders through my tee-shirt.

'Oh, my God,' she said softly, out of enjoyment.

She shifted position, forcing her breasts more up towards my eyes, her second thigh going up my other hip, the skirt negligible now, wanting me so deep inside her. I felt the unmistakable opening of her hips, finally giving up suppressing my arousal, but both knew sex was not happening. This was love not sex. We kissed again, I ran my hand through that hair which had first caught my eye in the long bunches, and I smiled against her mouth, as both of us felt the drug of total happiness.

I almost said something not said for years, that I now loved someone. Her eyes fluttered at the aborted comment.

'So, you'll come away with me, then?'

'I'd love to.'

TWENTY-ONE

A few days passed without seeing Joely. I worked, enjoying the company of Tim and Nervo, agreeing with the latter to have him cover some of my shifts. During one tea-break, Tim had a visit from Beth where she updated him on their holiday plans. I was happy to see her, nevertheless putting down my favourite mug in case of fresh attack as she moodily glanced at me a couple of times. Before leaving Tim with a kiss she stepped into the office to silently hug me.

There was no Nichola or Karen around the place, and definitely no Molinas to face up to. Out on the sun terrace one afternoon, I had a good look around the grounds for them, Harry Madox patting me on the back and begging me not to jump. I smiled at him, savoured the refreshing air, then looked up at the rippling club flag, full of bird shit.

I walked through a staff door into Carla. She couldn't look at me, even trying to keep walking until I took her arm.

'Carla, baby, I thought we were all right again?'

'So did I, but...'

'Tell me, Carla.'

'Oh, I don't know.' She messed with her hair in an exasperated manner. 'Rachel Calderbank was talking to me about you. She said something that's confused me about you again.'

'I can't wait to hear this.'

She slowly wobbled her head while I waited for her to put the charge into words.

'She said,' continued Carla, 'that when you first came down here, you asked her to come onto your ex-girlfriend's new boyfriend. That you'd pay her to help split them up.'

Probably under different circumstances I would have been furious, but I just slowly smiled.

'She said that's why she doesn't like you.'

'And you believed her?'

We paused there while Carla mulled it over. I gave some consideration to doing violence to Rachel Calderbank. Gradually Carla's body language relented, and she moulded into my embrace. We hugged for longer than friends hug. I finally let her go and we gave each other the chance to speak, but nothing was necessary. She kissed my cheek before a gaggle of receptionists bundled her off to lunch. I watched her until she turned out of view.

My chance to confront Rachel Calderbank presented itself late in the afternoon outside the main reception. She was standing having a serious conversation with a member of her bar staff, close enough for me to have run across, got into her face, let the bitch really know my name. But then came the arrival of Tommy Macro and his visiting friend, Gus, who was smiling as always and engaging in banter with another person who he had won over with his wit and charm. On seeing Rachel Calderbank he was even more animated, until she suddenly smashed him in the face with a right hook, whip-lashing his head back and making him sink to one knee in great distress. Rachel Calderbank proceeded to berate Tommy Macro over whatever crime or slight his friend had perpetrated on her, then removed her waistcoat and threw it in Macro's general direction as she stormed off to find alternate employment. I watched the scene from outside my office with amused fascination, only unhappy that Tim and Nervo had missed it.

After the particular visit to Candlesby village that finished with bath time with Beth, we put on appropriately sized towels and lounged around near the door to cool off. I was making a move to get ice pops when the phone rang.

'Yes?' I listened into the handset and then said for Beth's benefit, 'Pitch and Putt, Tim. *Now*?'

She initially shook her head decisively, then under my stare she gave a "whatever".

'All right, then,' I continued. 'What's this obsession suddenly with golf? Oh, Tim, have you lost something?'

Beth followed my Audi in her battered Mini to the Council run golf course. While not exactly being the Augusta National, it was functional and fun, with trees and artistically designed sand traps, and a pub facing the park gates. I waited on the car park for Beth, coming to me smiling. I tidied her ponytail for her.

'You smell nice,' I told her.

'Thank you. So do you.'

As we approached a blue hut with the first tee and the eighteenth green we were spotted by Tim's older brother, Rob. He alerted Tim, who appeared with his nine-iron and putter to come jogging towards us. I kept on walking as Tim reclaimed his woman in a passionate clinch. I smiled at Tim's brother.

'They've dragged you out as well, Rob?'

He answered cheerfully, 'So it would seem.'

'Have we got time to get round?'

'We're last out. Go and get your clubs.'

Walking round to the hut window, I had the pleasant surprise of finding Carla practising her swing with her back to me. I paid for myself and Beth to a younger version of Nervo: somebody obviously driven mad by a summer of doling out balls and clubs. I had brought my own real golf ball which I dropped to the dirt and gently chipped into Carla's mini-skirted backside. She spun round.

'Nice form,' I told her.

'Hiya, you.'

'So, you're still here.'

'Not long now and I'll be out of your life.'

Rob led the way to the first tee, with Carla and I chatting intimately and Tim and Beth all over one another.

'Oh, this is great,' joked Rob. 'Has anyone got a magic marker? I want to write "I've got a girlfriend" on my tee-shirt.'

It was ladies to play first, Beth making a clean but short contact. Then Carla stepped onto the dusty mound and cracked her ball into the field where archery is practised.

'We're going to be here all fucking night,' said Rob.

I handed over my spare yellow ball and Carla did better next time. All the boys hit the green.

We went on round the golf course, Rob the only one keeping score, other players passing us on the adjacent holes. The early evening conditions were perfect out there with the two couples talking until having to part to play shots. On the fourth tee, Carla asked me where my girlfriend was, then smiled and cuddled me. Beth swore at another fifteen foot trundling second shot. Rob pulled his second shot into a wooded area, but held his tongue and set off to find it. Tim and Beth were snogging again. I sat down where I was. I was happy and calm when I considered what else I should be doing that evening instead of bathing Beth, and then watching Carla kneel down next to me.

'When will you be going back?' I asked.

'Next week. I was going to come and say goodbye.'

'I might be away.'

'Oh, I suppose this will be goodbye, then.'

'Carla, I'm glad there's no bad blood between us. That we can still be friends.'

'Of course we can. I'll always want to be friends, Alex. Hey, you can come and visit me. Will you do that?'

'Yes. As long as I don't have to speak to any "Uni" twats called Nigel.'

'I promise you won't.'

She looked away across the trees and when her eyes

returned she had suddenly become upset. She watched me waiting patiently for her to speak.

'I thought,' she said. 'I thought we'd get really closer this summer. And I feel, stupid for what happened with Macro. Oh, God, I can't believe I went through with that.' Her head dropped with the shame of it. 'Why couldn't it have been you? Why couldn't it have been you I made love with this summer? I mean, he was all right. He wasn't horrible or anything.' She shook herself in disappointment. 'I just wish it had been you.'

'We have tried. There's a mental blockage between us, remember. Friends and all that.'

'I know. Where did that nonsense come from? Shall we try again?'

'Well, if we both slice our shots at the tenth, the out of bounds is well hidden.'

'I'm serious, Alex.'

'Do you think we should?'

She laughed. 'God, we're at it again. All right, then. Don't make love to me. Just fuck me.'

'Young lady.'

'Just fuck me.'

She put her arms around my neck and we hugged there in the field until Rob hacked sweating out of the trees. I gave Carla a peck on the cheek and we levered each other up. Tim and Beth were still snogging.

'Game on, for fuck's sake,' called Rob.

The ninth hole was the most popular, a good distance dropping away dramatically to a rickety out of bounds fence and a brook beyond, heavily covered by trees. It was me to go first, teeing up with a practice waggle while waiting for two lads to putt out ahead of us.

'Are we in the boozer after this?' asked Rob.

Beth had clasped onto Tim, not wanting to delay having his body, but he was up for the pub so she relented to his wishes. When he freed himself I led him aside.

'Yes, Boss?'

'Your gaffe's empty, right?'

'Yeah, why?'

'Carla.'

'Oh, right. And that Joely bird might show up at your place.'

I had a vision of Tim's girlfriend in my bath tub, then nodded.

I watched the two youths putting aimlessly back and forth on the green below us. 'What are these dickheads doing?' Then I shouted, 'Oi! Get off the fucking green!'

Tim kidded with his brother, 'We're out with Alex. That means a fight.'

I lost my patience and played my shot, my ball causing the youths to duck and decide to move on.

'I thought you never got stressed,' Beth teased.

On the leisurely walk down to the hole, Carla and I were close together, with the slight gradient the excuse to hold each other around the waist.

Carla was very quiet as we got to Tim's house in Hounslow. I led her by the hand around the back and unlocked the kitchen door with the key given to me by Tim. With nothing to say we just kissed up against the kitchen unit. Taking a pause she looked through into the lounge.

'Nobody will arrive?' she asked.

'No.'

'Weird, Tim's house.'

'You think Tim's house is weird?'

'No, I mean it's weird that we're going to do it here.'

'Are we going to, then?' She shrugged and pulled a face in the affirmative. 'Right now? Shame I'm sober.'

She laughed. 'Thanks, Alex.' She investigated the hall. 'You're so flattering.'

'I meant I wished we'd been out drinking together first.'

We kissed in the hall next.

'It's all a bit staged,' she said, adding, 'but that's not a problem. Is it?'

My feelings for Carla, our previous false starts, not to mention a certain Joely, all combined to make me hesitate again. She pulled me down onto the stairs and worked on me with passionate kisses and roaming hands.

'Don't give me negative vibes, Alex.'

'I'm trying not to.'

She laughed again. 'We've got this beautiful, romantic, cold Semi-detached all to ourselves. I want you. You've got to get Macro out of my head. I'm not going back to Uni thinking of his foreplay techniques.' We both laughed at that. 'My God, Alex, I told you, just fuck me. We can make love when you come to see me.'

'You're making good sense.'

'Just do it. Do what you want to me.'

I led her up the stairs, not knowing which was Tim's room until I saw the large green cannabis drawing on the door. A quick inspection told me the room was not too unkempt. I stopped Carla in the doorway and her eyes turned up to mine as if awaiting instruction.

'Carla, you promise I can make beautiful love to you when I come and visit?'

'Of course.'

'Right, then.' I removed my arm barring her entry. 'Brace yourself.'

TWENTY-TWO

I had my feet up on the pool table as I looked out across the peaceful countryside, and with the last slurps of a banana smoothie, I came to the definite conclusion that on the free CD in my Sunday newspaper it was not Elaine Paige singing *Memory*. Mildly annoyed, I removed the disc and successfully launched it through the doorway as I went to check the weather.

Wiping my sweaty brow after a "pre-match" work-out and stepping into my boots, I found the lack of cloud cover distinctly disappointing. Nevertheless, the green cagoule went on. While looking for my shades, the phone rang. I stared at it and then almost ignored it.

'Hello?'

'Is that Alex?'

The female caller seemed agitated.

'Yeah, who's that?'

'It's Alison.'

'Who?'

'Joely's friend, Alison. Listen, she's having trouble with Oliver, you know, her Ex... He's taken her car keys. I've tried to get in touch with her dad...'

'Where is she?'

'She's here, outside. Can't you hear her shouting?'

'I'm on my way. Remind me, Alison, the name of your road.'

'Deane Street.'

I drove very quickly, forcing myself to listen to the radio, determined to stay composed and rational but fairly sure I would be beating the shit out of Oliver. I found Deane Street despite asking for directions from one of those meandering morons who like to include local history. Joely was in the road wearing a black skirt and a red blouse. I thought she was in an Arsenal top again before seeing some kind of logo on the back. I pulled up with a mini-skid and jumped out.

'Joely.'

She came towards me looking calm, a bunch of keys in her hand, the drama seemingly over. I touched her face with concern.

'Really, there was no need for you to come.'

'Has he gone?'

'No, if you listen you'll hear him over there in the flowers crying.'

'Jesus, Joely, what's with this guy? I understand the broken heart deal but he should be thinking straight by now. I'm gonna kick his head in.'

'No, you're not. Leave him alone.'

'Have you left him hanging on?'

'Of course not.'

'So, you've explained your feelings to him? Not just blanked him like a piece of shit?'

'Fuck, Alex, do you think I'm like that?'

'Right, I'm gonna kick his head in.'

'No!' She took a sled ride on my arm as I moved towards Oliver. 'Will you just go?'

I got a grip on myself. Her hair was in those bunches again, her face strained yet beautifully glowing. I determined to store that look away in my mind, bringing it out when it was my turn to cry in the flowerbed.

I saw a logo for a local Coffee House on her left breast.

'I didn't mean that,' she said. 'Come in.'

'What, and leave him there?'

'Come in.'

I finally saw Oliver, sitting with his head in his hands on a grass walkway between purple and pink flowers. I thought it really would be for the best to punch the lad a few times, to get him hating instead of moping. Joely had taken my hand, leading me into the house and into the living room. She held me, expecting a rejection, but instead she removed my tension. After a while she took me down onto the sofa. I pulled the logo on the blouse roughly away from her breast.

'I'm a barista, part-time,' she explained. 'I am a student, though.'

'Shouldn't you get to work? If Oliver's still in the plants I'll take him for a drink.'

Her full lips jumped to a pursed position as she fought back tears.

'Alex, please don't think of me as a bitch.' She started to speak quickly to communicate her emotions, 'I did everything right with Ollie. He's going off to the States and just got upset trying to say goodbye. Please, I'm not a bitch. I'm not.'

She cried and I almost cried with her, holding her close. It was a good cry, much better for it, her knees brought up to my chest.

Eventually she emerged and sniffled and tried to smile.

'You don't think I'm a bitch, do you?' she asked while I caressed one thumb across her lips.

I took my time, cupping her chin, softly kissing her once.

'Joely, I think I love you.'

'Shush,' she quietened me. 'Not yet. Tell me in a few days.'

I kissed her again. 'Why in a few days?'

'Because our flight's on Tuesday night.'

I digested that news in a mild panic, thinking I should be somewhere else, but found myself unable and unwilling to disturb the girl nuzzled against my chest. I gently stroked her hair, unconcerned that she was due at work and that Oliver was crying outside. When the moment mellowed she sat up, slightly bothered that her face might be a little puffy, telling me she would not be missed at the coffee shop when I tidied the part of the blouse with the logo.

'Stay with me,' she said.

She looked so innocent and vulnerable that I wanted to stay close with her. To stay with her in bed. I looked at her for a good few minutes, imagining unhurried intimacy and lovemaking, seeing her all supple and compliant, warm and pleased. I wanted to explore her entire skin and feel every movement of her body. Perhaps she was thinking the same things. Then I shook the thoughts from my mind, reminding myself that those feelings were for when we were away from that place. They were my prize.

'Let's do something,' she suddenly said. 'Something silly.'

I had to laugh and she came up with a luminous smile.

'Like what?' I asked. 'Paintballing? Shoplifting?'

'Swimming.'

'Swimming's not silly. Unless we do the synchronised bit.'

'Cycling.'

I smiled to myself.

'That's not silly, either.'

'I know, but let's go cycling.'

'I ride all the time.'

'Yeah, but not on a romantic trip with me.'

Before I could come up with a reason not to, she was off to get changed, calling that there were two bikes in the shed and she would ride the crap girly one. I stood to look out of the window, not seeing Oliver anywhere and pleased that my Audi had all its windows intact.

'Can we not ride past Oliver, if possible?' I asked.

'We'll go out the back way.'

I gave some consideration to watching her change, before she was there in Adidas leggings and white top, leading me out by the hand.

'God, I'm actually excited,' she said. 'I've not been on a bike for years.'

'Now, that does surprise me.'

'And what does that mean, Mr Rubber Toe?'

'Nothing. Where are we going?'

'Just round the village.'

Her bike was indeed crap in a shade of pink with

diagonal crossbar. I rode an old mountain bike behind her at first, amused at her bolt upright seating position and firm concentration on the road ahead, just like the way she drove her car. She looked back and smiled at me.

'We'll cycle when we're on holiday,' she called back. 'We'll tour the island.'

'The island? You're giving me clues.'

'Oh, we can't be doing that now, can we?'

I had to zigzag to retain my position while glancing at Joely's lower back, finding I was enjoying riding despite cycling having taken on a different meaning. It was a lovely day, not affected by Garage music banging out of a taxi firm's premises or the aroma of fish and chips in the air.

Joely put on a spurt before skidding to a stop on gravel.

'Loved to have seen you go over the top there,' I said as I went by, before u-turning to dock alongside her.

She smiled, looking all around. 'What do you think of my area?'

'What do I think of your area?' She playfully tried to stop a derogatory remark by making grabs at my groin. 'It's a toilet.' I fended her off as we laughed together, then she carefully balanced against me to kiss.

A noisy diesel van slowed near to us, with a builder's mate or some such person leaning through the window to cheekily call, 'Ee, ar, love. What are you doing with him when you could be with me?'

Joely found that hilarious, laughing even louder at my impotence as I watched in mock fury as the van disappeared up the road. Still laughing, she kissed away my indignant expression and took me into a hug.

TWENTY-THREE

The feeling crept up on me that Sunday night as I drove home from seeing Joely. It moved into happy thoughts of holidaying with the girl. Abject, all-consuming loneliness came over me, of course due to the enormous chasm between the good of Joely and the bad of what I was involved with. I drove without music, accompanied by the orange glow in the sky from the just departed sun. I felt grim, never more unhappy, the gloss put over the action I was taking had fallen away, the mental barriers that prevented evaluation of risk or consequence were gone. I knew it would have to be tomorrow. It would be over with tomorrow.

I parked up behind the Takeaway, planning a good meal, a good last meal. Yes, tomorrow I would take the risk and start living with the consequences. I was halfway up the stairs before I saw her sitting there. At first I failed to recognise the face. It was Kimberley from the Coffee Shop down the street. She was clearly in a distressed state, looking at me like a frightened wild animal. I was so surprised I just said, 'Hello.'

'Hello.'

I was prepared to wait for an explanation.

'I have got a good reason for being here,' she said. 'Well, it seemed like a good reason a few hours ago.'

'Do you want to come in?'

It wasn't cold, the evening had just become mildly uncomfortable. She stood in my flat with her arms protectively crossed. I noted the flip-flops and the plain blue dress. I started making coffee. She was out of luck if she wanted tea.

'I've had a terrible row with Marcus.'

I looked at her. 'And you thought it best to come here?'

'Well, I thought it best not to run home to "Mummy and Daddy" (she did the mime thing with her fingers) but, er, stay close to home, but, obviously as good as the moon to Marcus. Like I say, it was a good reason a few hours ago.'

I wandered behind her. She turned to look at me, still with her arms crossed. It certainly felt different having her there. There was only sex between us, not friendship like Carla, Beth etc. It was like this vulnerable woman was being offered up as a nasty bonus before I finally did the Devil's work the following day. She had goose bumps on her upper arms. She was biting her lower lip as if still expecting to be ejected. I locked the door.

'Are you hungry?' I asked.

'Yes, a little.'

We ate toasted cheese sandwiches as we sat in the silence of the flat. I deliberately kept the TV and the radio off and didn't bang on the wall with a request to Miss Brocklebank. I stared at Kimberley, letting her start to talk and she recounted the argument with Marcus and her flight down the street and thanked me a few times for giving her sanctuary. She booked a bath for after the meal and from her flitting eyes and frantic tucking of hair behind ears she was also thinking about how private that should be after my more than generous act. Or at least that was what I chose to read into her mannerisms.

'What's Marcus like?' I asked.

'Well, erm, normally he's a regular bloke. But there's a nasty temper streak there.'

'Really? I didn't see that, after we'd... behaved as we did.'

'That seems a long time ago now. Bloody hell, I used to watch for you coming in for your coffee.'

'Yeah, I used to like going in there. The coffee shop culture and what have you.'

'I've seen you sitting on your stairs many times. I wanted to come along and say hello. Obviously it wasn't possible.'

'We could sit out there now. Or maybe not. Shall I run your bath?'

'Yes, please.'

'Then what shall we do with you?'

'Whatever you like. I'm easy.'

I went to the bathroom and opened the taps before returning.

'You'll want to put something else on? What can I put you in?'

'Like I say, I'm easy.'

I handed her some never worn pyjamas as she coyly passed me on the way to the bathroom. She had an undisturbed hour in the tub while I watched Spanish football on Sky and then tried to decide on a film. She tottered out in her blue pyjamas with her head in a towel. Undecided where to sit I welcomed her down onto the sofa.

'Do you rub dry?' I asked. She murmured in the affirmative. 'Let me rub your hair.'

She put her feet up and turned away from me. I let her soggy locks fall free and began to towel her hair dry.

'That's lovely,' she said.

'I should think so, I used to be a top hairdresser.'

'Did you?'

'No.'

She tutted and settled back into me.

'What are we watching?' she asked.

'I don't know yet.'

She surfed the Movie channels. '*Notting Hill*, or Brad Pitt in *Snatch*, or Mathew McConaughey in *A Time To Kill.*'

'I don't fancy that one.'

I vigorously rubbed her hair.

I awoke on the sofa and wondered what time it was. I was convinced that it would all come together on that day. An early bird strike at Mathers was not possible with Kimberley as a house guest, but surely there had to be a rendezvous between myself and the man on that day.

I had showered and started breakfast when Kimberley surfaced, looking calmer and refreshed. She sat in my springy chair while we chatted and I got the impression she would not be staying much longer.

'That's a girl's bedroom,' she said.

'You reckon? Do you want some bacon and eggs?'

'No, thank you. I might do some toast in a minute.'

'Are you seeing Marcus?'

'Yes. Hopefully everything will be sorted out today.'

'I hope so too.'

A car pulled in down below, almost to be expected by then. I put the pan off the heat and excused myself, going out into the bright sunshine to see Joely jump from her Citroen.

'Don't panic,' she called, meeting me in an embrace halfway down the stairs. 'I just stopped by on my way holiday shopping to see if you needed anything.'

I was more interested in kissing her, the passion of the condemned man flooding through me. She accepted the early morning snogging session before playacting being flustered when I let her breathe.

'Well, can you think of anything?'

'No. Just get me anything you think I might need.'

'Right. I'll do that. See you later.'

My right hand moved through her hair and brought her head back for one last kiss, while my other hand rested on her warm bare lower back. Reluctantly I let her go. We exchanged waves, and then the Citroen disappeared up the alleyway.

Deliriously loved up, I stepped back into the flat, aware Kimberley was in the kitchen as my eyes adapted again. Kimberley's fresh, happy demeanour had vanished, leaning on the side as if for support. I think I started to register her thoughts before she spoke. A black shadow moved across my heart as if the Devil had embraced me.

'She's called Joely, isn't she?' Kimberley asked.

'Yes.'

I was pretty sure about it by then. Kimberley's horror was pungent.

'She's Marcus's cousin.'

I sat on my pool table because it was there. Kimberley just stood looking at me. I didn't think about it by using language, it just consumed me in a total and frustrating cruelty. I never cried but I had to blink to control the emotions. I looked at Kimberley. The silence between us communicated everything about a cuckolded husband and about revenge, about the maliciousness of a girl to play out a part so perfectly, to set me up for a huge fall. I continued to sit there staggered, imagining I should feel bereaved or furious, but I just felt empty. Kimberley remained where she was, it all being shocking to her life as well.

I thought about the fiction Rachel Calderbank had told Carla about my honey trap plan and contemplated how to harm Rachel Calderbank. Leaving her alone in Rachel Calderbank world would be punishment enough. I thought about how to harm Marcus? How to harm Joely? Harming... Joely?

Kimberley moved.

'Where are you going?' I asked.

She used the apostrophe gesture again. 'Mummy and Daddy's. I can't just stand here, sorry. Do you want me to say anything? I mean, right this minute?'

'No, Kimberley. What is there to say?'

When Kimberley had gone, I got ready in a daze to go to Candlesby. I drenched my head in cold water, drank half a pint of milk, put on the cagoule, the baseball cap and the shades. I put some biscuits and a carton of juice in the rucksack. It was a slow walk down the stairs. I cycled slowly out of the alleyway to find the village as normal and quiet as ever. I passed Mrs B in her usual place and saw the woman who walked as if pushing a wheelbarrow; then as I focussed on my front wheel turning over I visualised Joely that first time there on the street. As I neared the coffee shop I had no thoughts on the place, no plan about it. I could just as easily have speeded up and out of the village, but something made me stop and enter the premises. Still I had no plan; it was just instinct that made me go in and then spit on the floorboards instead of outside on the street. Two early customers were no doubt appalled, but I was focussed on Marcus before me, dressed as he was in all black and making no reaction to the defiling of his premises as he had not reacted to the defiling of his wife. Instead he stood glowering at me. I went for him; he meekly threw a jug at me and then he had the Full Andy Hartson Treatment up against a coffee machine with a crash of crockery and squealing departure of the customers. He sank down with a surprisingly neutral expression, neither terrified or about to explode. I pulled my head-butt, let him slip to the floor and walked out of the place.

I rode towards Candlesby, letting the exercise flush my mind and with adrenalin feeding my building anger. I was ready, more so than on my previous attempts. She had seen to that. I banned myself from thinking about her, but what she had tried to perpetrate moved with me like the shadow on the road.

The first visit up The Mount proved fruitless, and eventually I retreated a few miles seeking a place to eat and regroup. I opened up through the gears again with the smog mask flying behind me and the shades hooked into the cagoule's front pouch. An unknown village came around a bend so I stopped pedalling and cruised in, breathing hard, looking for a secluded spot to stop. Ahead on the left appeared the black and white scoreboard for a cricket match. Going past tall kerbside grass, I could see a group of lads having a tennis ball game of cricket out in the middle, so that was where I stopped to eat my biscuits, sitting just inside the boundary fence.

The feeling of loneliness hit me again. The lunacy, of both what I was doing and who Joely was. The lunacy, sitting in the company of strangers, picnicking, eating just for energy, hearing playful shouts that were my excuse not to concentrate on who Joely was. I looked down at the grass with my head in my hands, hearing more shouts and a run out and swearing, and swearing in my mind.

I looked up and watched the boys play. Deep breaths, I told myself. The lunacy was almost over. Surely the odds were now in my favour; one of the laps of The Mount would coincide with Mathers leaving his home. There was just a need to keep focussed through all the anxiety. I rested a while longer before heading back to Candlesby.

An ominous build-up of cloud welcomed my return to Candlesby. I clipped my mask in place, the shades already on. One of the houses had sprouted balloons and a banner proclaiming the 40th birthday of Kenneth. I wondered whether it would be a memorable one. At the disused Post Office I pulled up as a car could be heard. For a moment the obvious didn't register. I realised that the distinctive growl was that of Tina Molina's Chimaera just a second before the vehicle braked at the bottom of The Mount. Mathew Molina's free-spirited young wife had a quick look left and right before gunning the car away. I listened to the roaring engine until it was gone. Tina's face had been happily preoccupied, so much so that she had not even seen me, never mind recognise me. I briefly tried to imagine her liaisons with my man Mathers, and then I visualised Mathew Molina on that rainswept street in Walton-On-Thames, spouting all the nonsense about a threesome. The sound of the sports car faded away, leaving me aware of birdsong above me.

Once more I went up The Mount, the ground mottled with shade. I heard the air-brakes of a large truck down at the Cane factory, wondered if Mr Ed could be relied on to come across again. I didn't get that far. Blue Saab. Time slowed in just the realisation that the car's engine was running. Blood rushed home to the heart, jack-hammering against the ribcage, forcing me to have to concentrate on the basic functions of how to use my brakes, how to free the rucksack from my shoulders. The Saab was moving, so slowly, through each segment of the iron railings, gravel crunching, silver alloys turning. I managed to focus. Nothing else mattered. Joely didn't matter, there was nothing around me, it was tunnel vision now. The black handgun came out of the rucksack. Keith Jacques and Jimmy Sheridan had mentioned technical details but that was all forgotten, apart from how to slide off the safety catch before I let it sag into the pocket of the cagoule. The rucksack went back on.

The gate began to retract. I waited in limbo, the bike pointing back down The Mount, my right shoulder lined up ready to draw on the driver's window. The gate was halfway. I waited. The Saab waited. There were boisterous shouts somewhere near the factory, I heard the birds again, Mr Ed whinnied. The gate was three-quarters, the Saab started to inch out. Everything remained in slow motion for me, all my thoughts, imagining shattering glass, seeing a catalogue of film scenes with bodies juddering at the point of impact, but back to being imbecilic and ranking it alongside breaking someone's nose with a head-butt, refusing to recognise the magnitude of the act. My body felt it, however, adrenalin shaking my legs against the bike frame. My right ball followed the left up inside my body in the manner of a martial artist before a fight. Focus! I screamed at myself. It was all thought through – just carry it out.

Even as I recognised Mathers' face from the press cutting, the window down so no glass to shatter, reaching for the heavy gun, I knew there was a passenger. Knew there was somebody else, somebody in the blurred periphery. Maybe it didn't register until afterwards; maybe I didn't quite believe what I saw.

I think it was the hair I recognised, swishing off her beautiful face, as I pulled the trigger twice, point blank into Mathers' face.

Carla screamed and screamed.

Stranger on Stranger

CPSIA information can be obtained at www.ICGtesting.com
Printed in the USA
LVOW041027080312

272170LV00001B/315/P

9 780957 074507